RAFFLES' CRIME IN GIBRALTAR

by
BARRY PEROWNE

PRINTED IN GREAT BRITAIN
DEAN & SON Ltd.
41/43 Ludgate Hill   LONDON EC4

Published by DEAN & SON, LTD
© Fleetway Publications Ltd 1968

Made and Printed in Great Britain by Purnell & Sons, Ltd.
Paulton (Somerset) and London

603 03504 3

CONTENTS

		page
PROLOGUE	. . . . . .	5

Chapter

1.	CRIME IN TRANSIT	7
2.	NEXT DOOR TO CHUNDRA'S . . .	18
3.	END OF PAROLE	26
4.	THE EXTRA PASSPORT	37
5.	SUNSET GUN	48
6.	THE DEAD KNOCK ONCE . . .	58
7.	YELLOW HALF-MOONS	68
8.	AT THE BURNING GHATS . . .	79
9.	ALL CLUES VANISH	90
10.	KNIVES ARE TRUMPS	102
11.	THREE-THOUSAND-AND-ONE LOST SOULS .	112
12.	THE ITALIAN MAIL	125
13.	A SIGNAL FROM LAL CHUNDRA . .	139
14.	STAFF WORK	153
15.	THEY HANG THEM IN GIBRALTAR . .	166
16.	EXHIBITS A TO Z	176

PROLOGUE

THE place—Forge Park, Westchester County, U.S.A.; the estate of Andrew Payne Hulburd, millionaire.

The time—2 a.m., January 15th, 1937.

The man—Raffles!

Propped against a book on the big, carved desk, an electric flashlamp stamped a circle of white light on the door of the wall-safe. A brown, lean hand, the fingers delicately turning the dial of the combination, cast a shadow on the steel door. The light silhouetted one square, black-clad shoulder, and the outline of an opera-hat, jauntily slanted.

There was not a sound in the room; not a sound in the great house; not a sound from the vast grounds, with their scattered groups of laboratories and workshops. Night and winter held the estate of Andrew Payne Hulburd—promoter of scientific research and invention—in an iron silence.

The minute movements of the tumblers in the combination lock of the safe were audible—as the dial slowly turned—only to an acutely trained hearing, closely concentrated. Such as that of A. J. Raffles, cracksman, revolving the dial with skilled fingers, the tips of which had been sandpapered to an extreme delicacy of sensitiveness.

Twenty minutes from the commencement of his work on the combination, Raffles inserted a long, slender key in the lock of the safe-door, juggled the key for some seconds —and, with tense expiration of breath that fluttered the black silk scarf drawn up over his face to his eyes, pulled on the circular door.

It swung open.

5

As it did so, there shot across the room the white blaze of a torch that dimmed his own torch, there on the desk.

The cracksman turned like lightning.

The torch blazed into his eyes, gleaming blue between the slanted brim of his opera-hat and the top of the scarf that hid his face.

The torch was held in a hand that thrust at shoulder height between the drawn, heavy dark-red curtains of a window recess. A clear, cool voice said quietly:

"You are covered! Remove your mask!"

Raffles raised his right hand slowly to his scarf. His left hand, behind him, was gloved. He stood with his back to the safe. As with his right hand, he slowly drew down the scarf from his face, his gloved left hand, behind him, smoothed over the door of the safe smudging or obliterating possible finger-prints.

The torch between the curtains played steadily on his brown, lean, handsome face, his firm lips, and neat, black moustache. He was steel-tense, but cool. He slightly lifted one shoulder.

"A fair cop! Why did you bother to let me go so far?"

"Because," said the cool, clear voice from behind the curtains, "I heard you coming through that window, just when I'd given up the hope of being able to open that safe myself. I hid myself here. I watched you. You seemed very expert. You've opened the safe and I'm mightily obliged to you. Now, go—as you came! Go and go fast! Don't look back! I have confederates outside that I can bring here in ten seconds with a signal. Go—and keep right on going!"

"You're a crook!"

"I'm a crook," continued the cool, quiet voice—"here on the same errand as yourself! I'm obliged to you for opening that safe! Meantime, you have five seconds to get out. This is a spring pistol I hold—quite silent, very effective."

"You hold all the cards! I give you best," Raffles said. "Good hunting!"

He took up his torch from the desk, snapped out the

6

light, pocketed it. He drew his scarf over his face, moved quickly to the window by which he had entered.

The shaft of light blazing between the curtains of the window opposite followed his movements, then snapped out.

"Better not try any tricks," came the cool voice through the darkness.

"I won't," Raffles said.

He didn't. In the long run, it might have been better for him if he had!

END OF THE PROLOGUE

THE STORY

CHAPTER 1

CRIME IN TRANSIT

THE lean, hard-bitten, white-coated barman dropped a curl of lemon-peel into a tall, frosted glass, wiped his paring-knife carefully on a spotless napkin, and said:

"Well, gentlemen—last port of call."

One of the two men who sat on high stools on the opposite side of the small, curved bar nodded a shade grimly. He was a heavily-built, powerful individual, in white flannels, a blue double-breasted coat and a panama. His face was brick-red, blunt-featured, with a long taut upper lip, a tight mouth, and hard, slate-grey eyes. He said, reaching for his glass:

"It's been a long trip. Melbourne, Fremantle, Singapore, Colombo, Aden, Port Said and now Gibraltar. Shan't be sorry to get home."

"Nor me," said the barman. "Six solid months since I seen the missus and kids! Still, one thing, when you bin away on a long run, you're sure of a welcome. It makes gettin' home worth——" He caught the eye of the younger of his two customers, and his voice tailed off.

He added, with a touch of embarrassment: "Well, drink up, gentlemen—the next is on me. 'Bout time I bought you a drink, for a change."

He was a good chap, the barman, Harry. All the way from Melbourne, aboard the s.s. *Llandnno Chief*, these two men had been his best customers.

From the first, when they came aboard at Melbourne, there had seemed to him something slightly odd about them. They were so inseparable. They were like Siamese twins. They seemed friendly enough, but there was something between them that he found hard to understand.

It was as though they shared a secret that the thickset man, Mr. Marius, took much more grimly than his companion, Major Alan Bell-Evart. The major had a way of seeming to mock the elder man. You had the feeling, sometimes, that the major, when he was saying one thing, really meant another—something quite different. *Double entendre*, the French called it.

There was no doubt about it, the major had an acute sense of humour. It was difficult to put your finger on anything. It wasn't so much what he said, it was the way he said it. Very pleasant, you couldn't help liking him, but he had a way of drawing your attention to Marius, making fun of him. It was so subtle that you hardly knew he was doing it, but Marius knew all right; and as his blunt, square face turned a deeper and deeper shade of brick-red, you couldn't help but want to laugh.

There was no spite in the major's goings-on; it was just a sort of devilishness he had. He was a gentleman, you couldn't mistake that, and he had a quick, clever mind. Marius wasn't a gentleman, and he wasn't so quick that his wit would ever dazzle you. Marius was plain tough.

Queer travelling companions, Harry the barman thought them. Harry always spent the first four or five days at sea in weighing-up his smoke-room customers, getting to know who would be regular, and who, once the novelty of being at sea had worn off, would desert the smoke-room for the drawing-room or the lounge. It was soon plain to him that Mr. Marius and Major Bell-Evart would be regulars—and that of the regulars they were the most interesting.

It was queer how, from the beginning, in his own mind he had put Marius first. Whatever they were—business partners, was Harry's guess—Marius had the say about everything. The major might sign most of the drink chits, but what Marius said, went. There was no mistaking that.

Harry had got into an argument one night, a week out, with Sparks, the wireless operator, and the chief steward, the assistant purser, the second officer, and one or two others. It was late, the bar was closed, and they were having a quick deuch-an-doris on the sly. They had got to talking about the passengers, and Harry said:

"The couple that catches my fancy is them two, Marius and Major Bell-Evart. Can't make out what they are. As a guess, I'd say they was business partners—a gentleman sheep-farmer from up country, Forbes way, who's gone into partnership with his range foreman. I reckon the foreman—that Marius—knows the practical side, and the gentleman—that's the major—has got into the way of letting his partner have the say-so."

"Pretty good, Harry," said Sparks, "but that's not my guess. I've sat in my cabin sometimes an' watched 'em together on the sports deck. The major throws a nifty quoit at deck-tennis, he's always on for a bit of fun, but Marius never joins in."

"What's your idea, then, Sparks? Let's have it, Mr. SOS Blake, o' Baker Street!"

"Tell you," said Sparks. "The major's a remittance man, been down under for years—look at his colour: that sunburn's never skin deep. All right. He's recently come into his inheritance, back home, and the family's sent out their estate bailiff—trusted man—to fetch him back, and keep a tight rein on him to see he don't get some shyster to make him an advance on his legacy. They're afraid, if he did that, he'd get bottled in every port he touched, and land up home with the delirium tremens, or maybe never get home at all.

"You can see the major's always on for a bit of fun: that's because the baronial hall and the huntin' set is waiting to welcome him—bit different from the domain at Sydney—and he's full of the joys of spring. Marius is doling out a bit of money to him here, and a bit of money there, usin' the doin's as a lever to keep the brake on the major. Marius is only a servant of the family, see? He's got to keep his place, that's why he don't join in deck games with the major, but at the same time, just for this trip, he's got to keep the upper hand of him—in a respectful sort of way."

It was an ingenious theory, very nearly convincing to Harry; but he raised one or two objections, and that led to other theories being advanced, and a general argument.

But neither the chief steward nor the assistant purser took any other part in the discussion than that of opening another bottle of Bass apiece. Later, when the others were gone and Harry was boxing the empties for the boy to take down to his store, the chief steward, reaching for his white-topped uniform cap, said casually:

"Got you proper on a string, them two, Harry, ain't they?"

"For eight-'n-twenty years," said Harry, "I've been openin' up my bar as soon as we got outside the territorial limit, an' I've never yet had a passenger flummox me after the first week. But now these two, Marius and the major, have gone an' blotted my record. I'm provoked."

The chief steward adjusted his gold-badged uniform cap at a nice angle before a mirror on the wall of the tiny bar.

"Harry," he said, "you're gettin' old and beyond it. You're losin' your grip. You've seen their like time and time again."

"How's that, Will?"

"Under the hat," said the chief steward. "Only the old

man, and the purser's office, and me knows, and the old man'd keelhaul the lot of us if it got out."

"Under the hat it is."

"O.K.," said the chief steward, and winked. "Marius' full title is 'Detective-Inspector, C.I.D.' The major's his prisoner. Goodnight, Harry," said the chief steward. "Happy dreams."

A good chap, Harry the barman. He was astounded, but he never let the revelation make the slightest difference in his manner to Marius and the major. Already he liked the major well enough to feel sorry about the situation he was in.

He had to admit that Marius, hardbitten copper as he obviously was, nevertheless played the game. Not a hint of the true situation ever came from Marius. You would never have thought unless you knew enough to look for them, that he had a pair of bracelets in one pocket and a .45 in the other. But they were there. Harry, when he came to look for them, saw the slight bulges they made. Unmistakable.

It depressed Harry, but:

"That Marius is human. I don't like him," Harry said to the chief steward, "but you got to admit he's human. That's my idea of inferno, that is—pull a job, get clear away, right to the other end of the blinking world, and then they lag you, and you start back. Eh? Wake up every morning in your bunk, with the cabin full of sun and the sea sparkling, and maybe a day ashore ahead of you, a day's pleasant, decent drinking in some bars you never been in before, and then that grey feeling comes over you and you think: 'A day's march nearer Dartmoor!' "

"Gimme a Bass, quick," said the chief steward, "before you start me off sobbing."

"Makes you think," said Harry, as he poured the Bass, getting a nice spiral in the bubbles. "Made that Marius think, too, I reckon. That's why he's letting the major down as easy as he can—letting him enjoy this trip as much as can be expected. Lord, how I hate a copper, just can't help it, but still you got to admit this Marius is human, as coppers go.

"That's what had me deceived. I've seen plenty of coppers and copped in my time, and usually the copper takes his prisoner's money away; and usually the prisoner takes it harder than the major seems to. Usually they wallow in self-pity, ain't got no heart for anything—and Lord, I don't blame 'em! I've seen 'em try to drink themselves blind, and I've seen 'em try to go overside. But the major's different. He can take his drink or leave it alone. He keeps cheerful, he's got a sort of debonair way with him, and if he's a bit acid now and again, and maybe touches Marius on the raw, who can blame him? Why, a saint'd do it if that bloodhound Marius was always dogging round on his heels. I admire the major's guts!"

"Give it time," said the chief steward. "It's a long, long trail. Most of 'em start out chipper enough. They got the idea there's many a slip, and that's what buoys 'em up. A long voyage, anything might happen—ship might go down, and they grab a lifeboat and get washed up on some island not on the chart, where there ain't no extradition. That's what they think! They get all sorts of fantastical ideas, I bet. It's time that wears 'em down. Day after day passes, the old hooker logs her steady two-fifty or three hundred, nothing happens, and the Old Bailey gets nearer and nearer, and their hopes get fainter and fainter.

"That's what wears 'em down, Harry boy; and then you get your last port of call, and there's nothing left between you and retribution, Harry, but a day or two more at sea, with the weather gettin' a nip in it and the water turnin' grey. That's what brings 'em up against facts, Harry, and they know then that there ain't no providential desert islands, but only Dartmoor or the hangman. That's when they hit the bottle if they get the chance, or try to go overside. The major's chipper enough now, but wait till we touch Gib., last port of call. It'll be a different story then. Gimme a Bass—I'm a shaken man."

Inexorably, the *Llandnno Chief* flogged her way homeward. Marius and the major went ashore at Singapore, and Harry, the barman, leaning on the rail, watching those two duck-clad figures moving away through the colourful crowd of Malay and Tamils and Chinese coolies, while the donkey-engines clattered and the winches flashed bright in the burning sunshine, wondered whether something might not happen to those two, and whether he'd ever see them again.

But nothing happened, and Harry said to the chief steward that night:

"You can't get away from it, Marius is givin' the major a square deal all right. I never knew a copper yet that didn't lock his prisoner up while we was in port. But here Marius takes the major ashore with him!"

"The major may be a crook," said the chief steward, "but it looks as though Marius gives him credit for being an officer an' a gentleman. I reckon the major's given his parole not to make a break for it when they're ashore, an' Marius has accepted it. That's O.K., now—early days yet, and the major ain't had time to get really desperate."

But they went ashore again together at Colombo, and Harry, who had shore leave too, saw them riding in a rickshaw, and you would never have taken them, he thought, for detective officer and prisoner, not in a hundred years.

The *Llandnno Chief* made a fair voyage of it across the Indian Ocean, the bright days flickered by irrevocably, the ship's log showed her regular 270–300 miles run from noon to noon, and they came into the heat and torment of the Red Sea.

"This is where it begins to get 'em," said the chief steward. "It's the heat. Their nerves begin to get ragged. They start thinkin' about what's waitin' for 'em at home. They get a glimpse of land, and it's wild country, Arabia, and if they could get away there's a chance they could join up with some sheik and stay free for years. They begin to think about that——"

Sure enough, Harry several times saw the major leaning against the starboard rail, watching the far-off, scorched and barren coastline, as the ship beat her way up through the heat-blur into the region of the Bitter Lakes.

Sort of lonely, he looked, Harry thought—though Marius was sprawling in a deck-chair nearby, with a book on his broad chest, his eyes shut, and his mouth open.

The couple never mixed with the other passengers. Harry was the only person aboard they talked to to any extent. They played Russian Bank together for hours in the smoke-room every evening.

It was no use, you couldn't get to like Marius, even though he was treating the major with unusual humanity. At the same time, you couldn't help but like the major more and more. His nerve never showed a sign of cracking. Perhaps he poked fun at Marius, in that subtle way of his, a little more frequently, but there was no malice in it.

He was good-looking, the major—in his early thirties, not tall, but wellknit, with strength and grace and decision in his movements. He had a lean, brown face, his hair was dark and crisp, and his close-clipped, black moustache made his teeth look extraordinarily white. His eyes were full of vitality—reckless, humorous eyes, a keen blue. His white suits were always crisp and fresh; he looked cool, even going through the Suez.

Harry felt an extraordinary tension while they were in the Canal. He was acutely conscious of the flat, sandy banks off either bow; near enough to jump to, those banks looked. He saw the major, several times, leaning against the rail gazing at those banks slowly sliding past, and the desert inland with the quiver of the heat-blur over it.

At any unusual sound on deck, in the blue, hot night, with the stars hanging so low you felt you could touch them, Harry felt his heart contract. Anyone coming suddenly into the smoke-room brought Harry's head up sharply.

"I never felt like this before," he told the chief steward. "I can't help it, but in my heart I'd like to see him escape. What's he done, anyway? Murder?"

"Not that I know of," said the chief steward. "I've heard something about it being an American job he pulled. Robbery. Must have been a big affair: they say Andrew Payne Hulburd was mixed up in it."

"The American millionaire?"

"And inventor," said the chief steward. "Him and Edison was like that"—he crossed his fingers—"years ago. You often see pictures in the papers of the Hulburd estate—Forge Park, in Westchester County. Hulburd runs it as a sort of experimental station—a sort of science centre. Some inventor gets an idea, an' he's got no dough, so he goes to Forge Park and Hulburd puts a laboratory at his disposal and tells him to go ahead, money no object. It's a big thing, Forge Park."

"And that's where the major pulls his robbery?"

"So I hear, and if he's in the class that tackles a job like Forge Park, then he ain't no amateur, take it from me. They probably got a long list chalked up against him in England. Ain't your punkah workin'? It's so hot, I can hear my brains fryin' in my brain-pan."

"Is that what it is?" said Harry. "I thought I smelt onions."

The *Llandnno Chief* passed Ismailia, docked at Port Said. Marius and the major again went ashore. Some new passengers came aboard with them in the last tender—an English schoolmistress, an American girl, a Methodist missionary, and a young American who looked like a college boy.

Marius and the major seemed to have got acquainted with the American girl. She came into the smoke-room with them for a cocktail as the ship, sounding her siren, nosed out past the breakwater with is great statue of Lesseps.

She was gay and charming. It was a pleasure to serve her. Her name was Brook, Drusilla Brook. She was tall, for a girl, very slender and graceful, her skin golden-brown from the sun, her hair bleached by it so that it was very nearly flaxen. She wore it parted in the centre, dressed close about her head, smooth and shining, and her eyes were grey and they looked at you straightly and frankly. She had a look of race about her, and somehow she and the major seemed just right together.

They liked each other from the start, you could see that; and as the ship butted on down the Mediterranean, and the bright days flickered by, Harry felt more than ever sorry for Major Alan Bell-Evart. For though he never sought her out, they were attracted to each other, a blind man could have seen that; and it was obvious that Drusilla Brook wondered why Marius was always at the major's elbow.

The young American, who looked like a college boy, was also attracted by Drusilla Brook. He was tall and loosely-built, with blond, short hair, and the general cut of his jib put Harry the barman in mind of a younger edition of Colonel Lindbergh. He was on the passenger list as Dan Westray, junior.

Westray did his best to monopolise Drusilla Brook, but it was plain enough that, while she liked him, it was only casually, and her real interest was in the major.

Harry felt sick at heart when he thought of the situation the major was in. They were far down the Mediterranean by now. Less than a week would see them home. A police tender would be waiting on the docks for the major; a cell would be waiting for him.

Any hopes of a getaway which the major might have had would be gone now, Harry figured. The jig was pretty well up. If Harry felt sick at heart, how must the major be feeling?

Yet he remained as gay, as debonair, as ever.

"I can't help admiring him," said Harry.

"He's got more guts than most of 'em," the chief steward admitted. "Well, it's been a long trip, and it's nearly over. The purser told me that Marius made the pinch on Melbourne Cricket Ground. The major was sittin' there in his shirt-sleeves, watchin' a Sheffield Shield match. Melbourne Cricket Ground to the Old Bailey! Some trip, Harry, but it's all over now. Gibraltar tomorrow, last port of call, and then a straight run home. The major ain't got a hope, now, not a cat's chance. Retribution, Harry, my boy! It gets you sooner or later——"

A retribution, Harry couldn't help thinking, that must be made more bitter for the major by the presence of Drusilla Brook.

That was why Harry the barman could have bitten his tongue out when, just after the ship had anchored at Gibraltar, last port of call, and Marius and the major came in for a drink, he, Harry, had made that thoughtless remark about the pleasures of getting home after a long trip.

Considering the "pleasures" that awaited the major, he could have bitten his tongue out. It was with real embarrassment, a real sense of shame, that he changed the subject hastily with:

"Well, drink up, gentlemen—the next is on me. 'Bout time I bought you a drink, for a change."

The major smiled. For all the sign he gave he might not have heard Harry's unfortunate remark at all. He said:

"Why, thanks, Harry. Make it a quick one, then—tender's just going."

They made it a quick one, and the two went out together. Harry was surprised. He had not thought it likely that Marius would risk taking the major ashore with him at the last port of call.

Harry leaned on his bar and looked out of the window. He heard the deep boom of the tender's siren, saw the tender draw out from the ship's side, churn away across the sparkling water towards the shore. The Rock towered majestically above the bay; houses, lemon-yellow and blue and white, clung to the precipitous slopes; above the huddled houses was bare, naked, sun-hot rock; below them were the grey walls of the old bastions, and galvanised iron sheds along the quays.

Last port of call.

The tender dwindled away over the shining water, and Harry, with a sigh, turned to put his bar to rights.

Drusilla Brook came quickly into the smoke-room, just as he was about to pull down the bar shutter.

"Oh, Harry!"

17

"Yes, miss?"

He couldn't help admiring her—young, lovely, eager; and she seemed excited about something, he thought.

"Harry, has Major Bell-Evart gone ashore?"

"Just gone, miss."

"Is there another tender soon?"

"In ten minutes," said Harry.

He watched her hurry across the smoke-room and step out on deck. It never entered his head for a moment that he had seen Drusilla Brook, Dan Westray, Jr., Detective-Inspector Marius, and Major Alan Bell-Evart for the last time.

CHAPTER 2

NEXT DOOR TO CHUNDRA'S

MARIUS and the major stood in the shade of a big galvanised iron shed marked "Bland Line".

"Notice they've got the harbour boomed?" Marius said. "They don't take chances in Gibraltar. There's a war on. They're fighting over there."

"Over there" was the coast of Spain, making a wide arc of red, barren hills round the shining expanse of Algeciras Bay.

The major grinned. His clipped, black moustache made his even teeth seem extraordinarily white. He said:

"I can see how Spain, at war, is a darn sight too close for Gibraltar's peace of mind."

"Less than a mile," Marius said. "Gib's almost an island, but not quite. See that narrow neck of land yonder—flat, burnt, no trees nor nothing on it? That's neutral territory—'No Man's Land,' they call it. From the Gib gate to the Aduana of La Linea—that white building way over there, see?—is less than a mile. Once through the Aduana, you're in Spain."

"War or no war," said the major, "I'd rather be in Spain this minute than in your company, you big gorilla."

Marius' hard mouth cracked in a grim smile.

"I don't doubt it. But you gave me your word, or you wouldn't be ashore at all—not a cat's chance."

"You needn't rub it in," said the major.

The two men stood watching the thin trickle of passengers still descending the gangway from the tender.

The major lighted a cigarette.

"Considering this is my last port of call before—you know what," he said, snapping out his lighter, "how about doing something? You know the place, I don't. Where do we go from here?"

Marius' hard, slate-grey eyes had been scanning, not so much the passengers coming down the gangway, as the people who stood about on the narrow wharf in the shade of the great shed.

These were for the most part people with business there—a watchful policeman, blue-uniformed and helmeted, precisely like the London police; a few shipping clerks in light suits, carrying Board of Trade papers, manifests, bills of lading, and similar documents; a handful of ragged, swarthy individuals in blue shirts, berets, and rope-soled shoes—porters, these, guides, cabmen, of that race of Gibraltar multi-breed which sailors call "Rock scorpions".

At the major's question, Marius desisted from his scrutiny of these people.

"We can go where you like," he said. "There's the Rock Hotel, the Bristol, the Piccadilly Bar—those are the good class spots. There's the Royal, the Universal, the Suiza—they're cabarets: they go on all day when there's a ship in. Then there's the Monte Cristo, on Main Street: that's the spot I like best myself—next door to Chundra's."

"What's Chundra's?"

"Hey, are you kidding?" said Marius. "Chundra, Khitagara and Company, Hindu Stores—Tokio, Hongkong, Singapore, Calcutta, Colombo, Bombay, Aden, Jaffa, Acre, Alexandria, Limasol, Malta, Gibraltar. Why, they stretch clear round the world. There's hardly a town in the Near or Far East that hasn't got a Chundra store, or a store affiliated to Chundra's. It's a chain built up, owned, and managed by two brothers called Chundra. You never hear much about 'em, but they must be among the first fifteen richest men in the world.

"And powerful? Listen, just the other day, Mussolini—the Duce himself—closed down the Chundra store in Addis Ababa; said that it was an espionage centre, a clearing-house for anti-Italian information and propaganda. The Chundra brothers brought a little pressure to bear on the Duce, and the ban was lifted and the store re-opened inside a month!"

"I'd like to know how that was done," said the major.

The detective's smile was grim.

"So would Mr. Eden! But that's how powerful the Chundra brothers are. Yet you'd take their stores every time for nothing but the ordinary tourist-trap—brass trays, candlesticks, censers, fake antique stuff, imitation cloisonne; near-Persian rugs and near-Morocco leather, dud jewellery. Nearly all the stuff these bumboatmen sell, up and down the Mediterranean, the Red Sea, and Indian Ocean ports, comes from Chundra's. You'd be surprised if you knew how many Brummagem factories'd go up the spout tomorrow if Chundra, Khitagara & Company failed; and you'd be a sight more surprised—and so would a lot of people who think they know it all—if you got even a smell of the secret business in a score of illegal ways that goes on all over the world in the little private rooms behind Chundra, Khitagara stores."

"The C.I.D. knows more," sighed the major, "than anyone'd think from a look at its officers."

"I don't know half enough," said the dour Marius.

The two men had by now passed out of the shade of the shed. The sun blazed down fiercely. At a spiked gate at the end of the wharf, a man in white duck uniform and a pith helmet glanced keenly at Marius and the major.

"From the *Llandnno Chief*?"

Marius nodded.

"Staying in Gibraltar?"

"No, just looking round—going back on the last tender."

"O.K. Show your passports at the police office over there."

Horse-carriages—four-wheeled, top-heavy affairs with tasselled white canopies—and big Packhard, Buick, Studebaker and Chevrolet touring-car taxis were drawn up in a line outside the gates. Marius and the major walked past them, crossed the broad road, off which the sun glared blindingly, to the police office opposite.

A blue-uniformed policeman, without his helmet, sat in a small window. He took their passports, rifled through them. The major's bore a U.S.A. visa: rubber stamp marks showed, by dates, that he had been in the U.S.A. within the past three months. The policeman noted the numbers of the passports, but he did not stamp them. He handed them back, with a jerk of his head signalled both men through.

They walked down the broad road, low white warehouses to either side of them, the Rock looming gigantically ahead. Marius held out his hand, rubbing his thumb and forefinger together suggestively.

"I let you have it to go ashore," he said, "so no one'll start wondering. Once ashore, I'll take charge of it—as usual."

The major shrugged, handed over his passport.

They crossed some railway tracks and a small busy square with a clock tower in the centre; passed under a bridge marked THE OLD WATER GATE; flanked on their left a barrack square on which a squad of defaulters was parading, sweating in kilts and khaki drill tunics, and entered Main Street.

Very narrow, jammed between tall houses with their upper windows balconied and shuttered, crowded with cars and pedestrians, the street sloped up steeply before them.

The narrow chasm held the heat; the air quivered with it. Tourists and sailors in white, soldiers in khaki, Gibraltarians in dark clothes—all jostled each other on the pavements. Negroid Moorish hawkers, in white and khaki jellabies, with hennaed heels protruding from their

21

slippers, peddled picture-postcards and mementoes in the gutters. Hindus, neatly and coolly garbed in white suits, solicited custom from the rug-hung doorways of their tourist-traps.

There were three such scouts soliciting from the doorway of Chundra, Khitagara & Co.

"That's Chundra's there," Marius said, and turned into an alley which flanked the Hindu store on one side. "And here's where we get a drink—and I can do with it!"

The Bar Monte Cristo faced the side of the Hindu store across the alley. A bead curtain hung in the doorway of the bar. Marius held the curtain aside for the major to enter. It was dim within, and cool, after the glare outside.

"That door to your right," said Marius.

The major stepped through another bead curtain into a small room with a huge Moorish chandelier, rush mats on the floor, a few low Moorish tables and deep, low cane chairs scattered about. The room was empty.

Marius lowered his bulk into a creaking cane chair facing the window. He pushed his panama back from his seamed forehead, blew out his red cheeks, clapped his hands loudly.

"What'll it be?" he asked. "Whisky?"

"And ice," said the major.

A waiter in black trousers and a white, three-cornered jacket entered softly, saying:

"Senores?"

Marius gave the order. With blunt fingers he tore the cellophane from a packet of Gold Flake.

"The only quiet spot on Main Street, this," he said. "You can relax here. Cool, too."

The big window was wide open. The sill was raised only a foot above the floor. The alley on this side was in shadow. It was indeed pleasantly cool. On the opposite side of the alley, the sun shone; it struck brilliantly through a similar window, also wide open, at the side of the Hindu store. That room over there was full of glass showcases; its walls were hung with rugs, with Moorish slippers, leather cushions, pouffes. There was nobody in it.

"You'd think they'd be afraid of getting their stuff pinched," said the major. "Anyone could nip in through that window. I could flip my cigarette end through it from here."

"Nobody ever yet pinched anything from Chundra's," said Marius, "and got away with it. Hallo, here's the drinks. Aah!"

He smacked his lips. The waiter set down a tray on the table between the two men, withdrew softly, and Marius picked up his tall glass, tinkling with ice.

"I've hated to do it, major," he said, "but duty's duty. The least I can wish you is a just judge. Here's to him."

"The C.I.D. always gets its man," said the major philosophically. "Cheers, inspector."

They drank. The major was the first to set down his glass. As he did so a young Hindu, dark and slender, in a neat white suit with a narrow black tie, entered the room across the alley. He glanced over casually towards the room where the major and Marius sat—and he stopped dead. He stood for a second motionless, looking at them, then turned sharply and with a step vanished from view.

The major looked at Marius. His head was tilted back. It was another second before he set down his glass, empty, and exhaled with satisfaction.

"Taken and wanted," he said, and clapped his hands.

The waiter slid in to take a repeat order.

The major held his lighter, first to Marius' cigarette, then to his own. The major's eyes were expressionless. Marius, he believed, had not seen the quick entrance and exit of the young Hindu in the room across the alley. Yet that sharp look of interest on the Hindu's face had not been casual. It meant something.

The major leaned back in his cane chair.

"So that's Chundra's," he said. "Know anybody there?"

Marius' eyes hardened.

"Why do you ask? Want me to wangle you discount off some mementoes or something?"

The major was looking over into the room across the

23

alley. As Marius spoke, the young Hindu returned to that room. A gesture of a slender, dusky hand indicated to someone who followed him, the glass-paned show-cases. The Hindu's teeth flashed white in a salesman's smile. Next moment, a girl in a white linen costume—a slender girl, hatless, with golden-brown skin, and smooth, blonde hair parted in the centre—appeared in the major's line of vision.

The major said gently, answering Marius' question:

"I wasn't thinking of discount for myself so much as discount for a fellow-passenger."

He waved his cigarette, and Marius looked over at the room across the alley. He grinned.

"The charming American! Well, well! A butterfly in Chundra's web! They'll fleece her clean in ten minutes and send her off with a double armful of junk."

The Hindu was talking to the girl, pointing out this and that to her in the show-cases. Once he glanced across the alley, and the whites of his eyes showed oddly in his dusky lean face. He went on talking to the girl.

He opened a show-case, held up a string of amber beads for her to examine. The beads swung, flashing richly in the sunshine, from his slender fingers. But the girl, Drusilla Brook, shook her head. She said something —neither hers nor the Hindu's voice was audible across the alley—and accompanied her words with a little gesture of dismissal.

The Hindu tilted his head to one side, lifted his shoulders, and, returning the beads to the show-case, left her alone in the room. She walked slowly along the rows of show-cases, examining their contents. She had not, as yet, glanced across the alley.

Marius chuckled.

"There's a room out at the back of that place that, if she could see it, it'd raise the hair on her head. There are four old Moors in it, who do nothing else but unpack brasswork from Birmingham, rub dirt and dust into it, and polish it up with beeswax. It comes up like antique stuff."

"And you sit there," said the major, "and chuckle! C.I.D. gallantry! I'm going across to warn her not to spend too many of her good U.S. dollars in Chundra's."

"Yeah, and take her to tea at the Rock Hotel afterwards! All right, my boy—it's your last port of call. Make the pace while you've got the chance, before she knows where you're headed for!"

The major rose, walked across to the bead curtain in the arched doorway, paused there to light a fresh cigarette. Behind him he heard Marius' chair creak as the massive detective rose. The major clicked out his lighter, swept aside the bead curtain, and, saying "Come on, if you're coming," glanced back at his companion.

Marius, standing, was stooped a little over the low table, leaning heavily on it with both hands, his back to the big, open window, the blunt fingers of his right hand gripped about his glass.

It was the attitude of a man who, rising, had stopped for a second to finish his drink.

But as the major glanced at him, Marius' head bowed forward slowly on his chest, his glass broke under sudden pressure from his fingers, he coughed painfully, and a rush of blood came from his mouth.

The major stood for an instant stockstill.

Marius swayed.

The major, letting the bead curtain swing to, moved so quickly that he caught the lapels of Marius' double-breasted coat before the big man fell.

The major held the detective saggingly upright with lean, strong hands, speaking harshly:

"What is it, man? You're ill!"

The detective, knees buckling, head lolling forward, was a dead weight in the major's arms. He wrenched the man round, lowering him into a cane chair. Something prevented his leaning back normally. The major pulled him forward. From between the detective's shoulder-blades protruded the ivory hilt, carven into the likeness of an elephant's head and trunk, of a stiletto.

25

The major snatched his hands away, stepping back as though a whip had lashed his face.

Marius fell awkwardly back, and to one side, in the cane chair. His head lolled limply over the arm; his hands dangled, almost touching the rush matting on the floor.

The major, in white ducks and panama, stood as still as though lightning had struck him. His eyes were fixed on the elephant-head stiletto hilt protruding from the detective's back.

Suddenly the major turned his head, to look across the alley into that room at the back of Chundra's store. The sun glared in aslant on the show-cases, the walls hung with leather cushions, pouffes, brilliant shawls, rugs.

The room was empty.

CHAPTER 3

END OF PAROLE

FROM Main Street, nearby, came the high toot of bulb-horns, the throaty warning of klaxons, the indeterminate medley of sound from a populous street. Over all this, thin and far soared the cry of a bugle.

Yet this room seemed quiet—quiet and dim and cool, with its bead-curtained doorway and wide-open window, its ornate Moorish chandelier, its rush-matted floor, small tables, cane chairs, and its murdered man.

Its murdered man——

The individual who called himself Major Alan Bell-Evart turned his eyes from that room across the alley, looked again at the massive figure in the chair, at the hilt of the stiletto ivory-white between the broad, blue-clad shoulders.

Then he did a strange thing, this Major Bell-Evart. He raised his brown, lean hands and looked at them, first the palms and then the backs. They were tremorless.

The immense effort of will entailed by that, and by the

control of the sudden rush of blood to his head, and the violent knocking of his heart, did not betray itself in his face.

His mind worked with the quick, accurate flicker of film through a projector:

He was a criminal under arrest, en route to trial. This was the last port of call before Southampton and a police tender. Alone in this room ashore with his captor, his captor had died—stabbed, murdered.

What chance had he to be believed, if he presented himself before the Gibraltar authorities with the story that Marius had been stabbed by a third party, through a window open on an alley?

The major stepped suddenly to the window—only now did it occur to him to do this—looked up and down the alley. To the right, people on Main Street passed to and fro across the alley-mouth. To the left the alley dipped sharply, giving on a narrow back street; a shop marked Paneria—Bakery faced the alley across the back street; some men in blue shirts, rope-soled shoes and berets sat on flour-tubs before this shop, smoking, scratching themselves, talking. There was not a soul actually in the alley.

What were his chances of being believed? They were two—both perilously slender. The first was that the elephant-head hilt of the stiletto might bear the finger-prints of the soundless killer. On the other hand, he might have worn gloves, or held the weapon in a handkerchief. Such, then, was one chance—scarcely a chance at all.

The second chance was that the girl, Drusilla Brook, in the room across the alley, might have witnessed the murder. She had been in that room a second before it happened. Why had she vanished so suddenly? Had she seen what happened? Had she run out through the Hindu's shop to raise instant alarm? Or had she left that room quite normally, seeing nothing?

Impossible to know! If she had witnessed the killing, nothing on the face of the earth, it seemed to Major Bell-Evart—save only that questionable point of the fingerprints—could clear him of the murder of Detective-Inspector Marius, C.I.D.

He stood there rigid. If the girl had run out to give instant alarm, surely by now she would be returning with police? There were plenty on Main Street. There was one on duty outside the post office, actually adjoining Chundra's. A minute—a minute and a half, at the outside—should have sufficed to fetch him.

The major estimated that approximately a minute and a half had now passed since the blow was struck.

He listened intently. The normal noises of Main Street reached his ears. There was no sound of approaching footsteps.

The major faced his problem with a coolness possible only to an experienced criminal. An average man, so placed, would instantly have lost his head.

The major could himself raise the alarm. If he did so, his hope of acquittal rested on the possibility that there might be fingerprints on the elephant-head hilt, and on the possibility that Drusilla Brook had witnessed the murder. But there might be no fingerprints on the hilt, and the fact that no alarm had been raised seemed to indicate that the girl had left the room opposite a fraction of a minute too soon to witness what had occurred.

His chances of acquittal, if he himself raised the alarm, then, were about 99 to 1 against. And even if acquitted on the murder charge here in Gibraltar, he faced the virtual certainty of ten years' imprisonment in England on the charge for which he had originally been arrested by Marius.

The alternative?

His parole, which he had given Marius—his promise not to attempt escape while ashore—obviously expired with the detective's death. He could make a bid for freedom. If recaptured, the fact that he had attempted a getaway would seal his fate. He would hang. On the other hand, if he were not recaptured, he would escape both charges.

Clearly, fate had weighted the scales for the man who called himself Major Bell-Evart. There was only one course open to a man in his sane senses.

The major took it.

First he assured himself that the room across the alley was still unoccupied; then he pulled the chair, with Marius in it, a little to one side of the window. He put a cushion behind Marius, so that the stiletto hilt sank into it when he laid the man back in a more natural attitude.

Marius' white collar and his chin were bloodstained. The major flipped the handkerchief from Marius' breast-pocket, shook out the folds, so placed the handkerchief that it covered both Marius' face and his bloodstained collar. Now he looked like a man sleeping.

Constantly the major's blue, keen eyes flickered between the window across the alley and the bead curtain of this room.

A shuffle of rope-soled sandals sounded in the alley just at the moment when the major, stooping over the dead man, slid his fingers into Marius' breast-pocket, brought out his—the major's—passport.

The major straightened instantly. He yawned, patting his mouth lazily with the passport in his right hand, and with his left he reached for his glass.

A man passed the window, looking in.

The moment he had gone by, the major jammed his passport into his breast-pocket, whipped out his own handkerchief, polished the glass, set it down—holding it carefully with the handkerchief between the glass and his fingers.

There was a pool of liquor on the Benares brass top of the table, with fragments of glass in the liquor; and there were some blood spots visible.

The major lifted the table quickly into a shadowy corner, polished it wherever he had touched it, lifted another table up beside Marius, transferred his own glass from one table to the other.

He glanced quickly over the result of his labours, looked across at the still unoccupied room opposite, turned abruptly and walked to the bead curtain.

He swept the curtain aside, passed through into the dim passage, sharply clapped his hands.

Like a ghost the waiter appeared instantly out of the shadows. The major took out his wallet.

"My friend's sleeping," he said, and smiled, making a suggestive lifting gesture with his elbow. "Don't disturb him. I'll be back for him later."

He gave the man a note from his wallet. It was a Bank of Gibraltar note, with a picture of the Rock on it, for one pound sterling. The waiter glanced at the note, beamed, glanced through the bead curtain at the man with the handkerchief over his face, and nodded vehemently.

"Si, si, senor—esta bien."

He held aside the bead curtain of the outer doorway, and Major Bell-Evart emerged from the alley.

He felt ice-cold, yet his shirt between the shoulders was clinging wet with perspiration. His heart, now that the first stage of the ordeal was over, was knocking in his chest like a sledgehammer. He took off his panama, wiped his forehead, replaced the hat, slanting it jauntily, and lighted a cigarette.

He noted with satisfaction that his hands were still steady.

He crossed over to the sunny side of the alley and, drawing great lungfuls of tobacco smoke, walked up to mingle with the crowds on Main Street. The concentrated glare of the sun was somehow a relief to him after the dimness of that deadly room. He drifted with the crowd, moving gradually down the slope of Main Street.

Open touring-cars, packed with his fellow-passengers from the *Llandnno Chief*, passed each other—with not more than an inch to spare, because of the extreme narrowness of that channel of traffic between the tall, flat-fronted buildings—and white canopied horse-carriages, also loaded with tourists, clip-clopped to and fro.

Major Bell-Evart was unconscious of it.

He was trying coolly, calmly, to appraise his situation. It was about as bad as it could be.

He knew, actually, more about Gibraltar than he had allowed Detective-Inspector Marius to believe. It was perhaps the worst place on earth in which to be a fugitive.

It was not in the ordinary sense a town; it was a fortress. Its area was acutely restricted, and of that area whole sections were banned by the military, guarded by sentries.

There were two ways of leaving Gibraltar—one, by sea; the other, by land into Spain. But Spain was riven by civil war. Nobody, it was certain, could hope to pass into Spain, through the Aduana of La Linea, without special visas and permits. These the major was in no position to obtain. He had only his ordinary passport.

He wondered for a moment if it might not have paid him to have stolen Marius' passport and warrant-card; but he dismissed the thought. It was improbable that they would have helped him much, and, if he were retaken, his possession of them would have told heavily against him.

He reckoned that, with luck, it should be at least a couple of hours before that waiter disturbed Marius, found him dead, raised the alarm.

How was he, the major, best to take advantage of that two hours' grace?

He dared not make a mistake. At all costs, he must hold firm to his coolness of mind. He must not panic.

He saw a sign on his right—Piccadilly Bar. He passed, out of the sun-glare and din, into the shadowy coolness, sat down at a small table, ordered coffee.

As he sipped, thirstily, the black, hot beverage, it occurred to him suddenly that Marius might have died, not from the thrust of a stiletto, but from a stiletto skilfully thrown.

His mind fastened instantly on the picture of that young Hindu entering the room in Chundra's, across the alley; the Hindu's sharp look of interest as he had caught sight of Marius and the major; the way the Hindu had left the room at once.

Suggestive, that!

But the Hindu had returned to the room with Drusilla Brook. He had left her alone there. Certainly she had been alone in that room across the alley only a few seconds before the blow had been struck.

Which suggested the possibility that the American girl had herself thrown the stiletto—if it had, in fact, been thrown—and slipped away instantly. Which would, in turn, account for the fact that no alarm had been raised.

The major pondered that, dismissed it. He could not believe her guilty.

But neither could he dismiss a growing conviction that the elephant-head stiletto had been thrown, not thrust. And if his conviction were right, then it had been thrown from that room.

And now the major remembered how Marius had spoken of Chundra, Khitagara & Co., the things at which he had hinted—"secret, illegal business". Was it possible that Marius was engaged in some investigation of Chundra, Khitagara—that therein lay the motive for his murder?

It was possible. It was even probable. He was on to something, the major thought. But how could he make use of it to help himself out of the deadly dangerous salient he now occupied?

Pondering that problem, the major became aware of a figure beside his table. He looked up. It was a thin, swarthy man in a washed-out blue linen suit, a beret, rope-soled shoes. He carried a large basket covered with a snow-white table-napkin. A corner of the napkin was turned back, showing the fresh, bright pink of crayfish beneath. He had been going from table to table, trying to tempt people to buy these. He had had good success, for it was now that hour of the afternoon when the Gibraltarian business man takes his aperitiva.

"Mira, senor—fresca, gorda, muy buena!"

The major shook his head. The crayfish pedlar leaned closer, his tone changing, dropping to a whisper:

"Follow me, senor!"

The major looked at him sharply.

The pedlar smiled, with a flash of white teeth in a beard-stubbled countenance, tucked the napkin back over his crayfish, shrugged, said aloud:

"You no like-a? Pues, senor—adios."

But his eyes, as he turned away, signalled an urgent message.

The crayfish pedlar went to one or two more tables. The major remained tautly in his chair, his eyes following the man.

The major knew nobody in Gibraltar. He was mystified. He was suspicious. To follow this man might be dangerous. Not to follow him might be to throw away some possible advantage.

The major looked at it thus: To increase his present danger was almost impossible. To let slip the slightest glimmer of help would be madness.

Again, for Major Bell-Evart, the scales were unequally weighted. There was only one thing for him to do.

When the crayfish seller walked to the door and, for a moment, stood there framed against the sun glare and the ebb and flow of traffic, the major beckoned the waiter, paid him, sauntered toward the door.

The crayfish pedlar stepped out into the street, turned to the left, up the slope. He walked unhurriedly. Once or twice he stopped people on the pavement, twitching back the napkin over his basket to display his wares. He sold none.

The major's throat tightened, grew dry, as they approached the alley which contained the Bar Monte Cristo. When the crayfish pedlar crossed the road at a point a little below the alley, the major, with a cold shock, thought that the man was heading for the bar.

The major hesitated, his heart hammering.

The crayfish pedlar crossed the road and entered the store of Chundra, Khitagara & Co. The major stood on the kerb opposite, lighted a cigarette. He snapped out the lighter. With the feeling of a man diving into an ice-cold pool, he crossed the road and walked into the store.

The crayfish pedlar stood at one of the glass-topped counters displaying his wares to a fat Hindu in white ducks. The Hindu said, impatiently:

"No quiero, hombre, no quiero—anda, anda!"

33

The crayfish pedlar shrugged and turned away. He looked at the major, made the slightest backward movement of his head—which the major construed as a signal to stay where he was—and walked out of the shop.

A good many customers were in the place—mostly bronzed, white-clad tourists off the *Llandnno Chief*. They were examining the pseudo-barbaric, worthless jewellery, the shawls, rugs, leather-and-brass work in which the shop dealt.

The staff was all Hindu. There were seven or eight salesmen, all busily occupied with customers. The major did not see the slim, young Hindu who had looked so strangely at Marius and himself across the alley. But he saw someone else—Dan Westray, Jr.

The tall young American caught the major's eyes, grinned, and with his long, loose-limbed stride came across to him. The major cursed blackly in his heart—but his smile was friendly.

"You, too, Westray? We're all alike. We know it's junk, but can't resist buying it."

"That's right," Westray agreed. "But I'm not figuring on buying anything this time. I'm just waiting for Miss Brook."

"Oh, is Miss Brook here?"

The major's surprise was well-feigned.

"Sure," Westray grinned, "and she seems to be camped here, at that. I saw her come in, and came right in after her. She was just going into some room at the back of the store there, and I've been waiting for her to come out. She's certainly taking her time!"

The major was tense with an interest not betrayed in his tone.

"You'll look pretty funny if she's walked out without your seeing her—while you were looking over those rugs, or something."

"Not a chance," Westray said. "I know she's still in there somewhere."

At that moment, one of the Hindu salesmen coughed discreetly at the major's side.

"You please come now, sir. The cloisonne you wish to see, it iss in back room here. It iss veree good cloisonne —oah, assuredlee you will like thiss cloisonne, sir. Please come."

"If you see Drusilla in there, major," said Dan Westray, "don't tell her I'm lying in ambush for her. She's apt to duck me, if she gets the chance."

"I'll bear it in mind," said the major.

He followed the Hindu across the shop, down a narrow gangway between glass-topped counters.

Many questions were vibrant in the mind of Major Bell-Evart. He did not know what to make of this business of the crayfish pedlar. He could imagine only that his theory of the stiletto thrown from the room in Chundra's was correct; that his disposition of Marius' corpse had been watched from Chundra's; that the crayfish pedlar had been posted to wait for him to leave the Bar Monte Cristo, follow him, accost him at a convenient moment, bring him back here to Chundra's. If this were so, then presumably he was about to interview the murderer of Detective-Inspector Marius.

But why? What could the murderer want with him?

Another problem which deeply mystified Major Bell-Evart arose out of his brief conversation with Dan Westray, Jr. According to Westray, Drusilla Brook was still here on the premises of Chundra, Khitagara & Co. Where, then, had she gone when, a matter of seconds before the murder of Marius, she had left that room where the major had seen her? And why had she left that room so very suddenly?

The major was acutely suspicious, intensely alert, as the Hindu swept aside a bead curtain at the end of the gangway between the show-cases.

"You enter, please."

The major looked stonily at the Hindu.

"Enter yourself."

The Hindu shrugged and ducked through the curtain —and the major followed very quickly.

He found himself in the room opposite the Bar Monte

35

Cristo. The fat Hindu smiled at him, with a gesture toward the window.

"See," he said, with a strange, soft hiss in his voice, "how soundlee your friend sleeps, sahib."

Looking at an angle across the alley, the major saw Marius sprawled in his cane chair, the handkerchief over his face. The sight of the dead man, seemingly so peacefully asleep, had a macabre, a ghastly quality. It turned the major cold. He swung round on the Hindu—and stood stockstill.

The man was holding up, open, a flat, leather case, lined with red plush. The case contained a thin, deadly stiletto of tempered steel, with an elephant's head and trunk for its ivory hilt. A depression in the plush marked where a companion weapon had once rested.

The major's hand shot out.

The Hindu snapped the case shut, whipping it behind his back.

"Oah, no!" He smiled fatly, his teeth flashing white in his dark, heavy face. "But you will agree, sahib, that some small conversation with my employer will not be time wasted?"

The major moistened his dry lips.

"Your employer?"

"Nanda Lal Chundra, sahib. He back!"

Quick as the warning, the Hindu laid a hand on the major's arm, jerking him to one side of the open window.

"See, sahib?" The Hindu stared across the alley, a hand tight on the major's arm. "Watch, if you please."

In the cool dimness of that room in the Bar Monte Cristo, there was a glimmer of white. It came close to Marius' chair, stood motionless for a moment behind it. The white glimmer was the jacket of the waiter. With a quick movement the man came to the window, stood looking across the alley into the room in Chundra's.

The Hindu's hand pressed the major back against the wall.

In the room opposite, the waiter leaned suddenly from the window, glanced up and down the alley. Turning back into the room, he picked up the glass from the table beside Marius. As he did so he deliberately, but lightly, jogged Marius' knee. Marius did not stir.

The waiter put the glass back on the table. Stooping over Marius, he slid a hand, with extreme stealth, into Marius' breast-pocket, brought out the detective's note-case. As he did so, the corner of the case caught the handkerchief dangling over Marius' chin, twitched the handkerchief from his face.

The sneak-thief stepped sharply backward, staring in unspeakable horror. The note-case dropped from his hand. Suddenly, terribly, he screamed aloud, and, turning, vanished—running.

The Hindu, with a quick movement, stepped before the window and, reaching out, drew together the shutters. The room here dimmed. The Hindu turned, outlined against the strips of sunshine which penetrated the slats of the shutter.

"Decidedlee," he said, with that soft hiss in his voice, "the alarm iss now up! Within twenty minutes the fortress of Gibraltar will be mobilised for your capture, Major Alan Bell-Evart! Or should I say"—his voice dropped a tone—"Mr. A. J. Raffles?"

CHAPTER 4

THE EXTRA PASSPORT

THE sailing of the s.s. *Llandnno Chief* was delayed on representations from Inspector Sacarello of the Gibraltar police.

The chief steward heard it from the purser, and he went along to tell his friend, Harry, the barman, that sailing was to be delayed.

"How long?" said Harry.

"Indefinitely. Purser says the Old Man's so mad he could chew wire nails."

"What's doing, then?" said Harry.

"I dunno. It's a police affair. I reckon the major's mixed up in it?"

"Why?"

"We was due to sail at five. Last tender from the shore was four-thirty. It's just come alongside. All the passengers are aboard—except four. Miss Brook and that young Yank, Westray, who joined us at Port Said, and the major and Marius. My belief is, the major's ducked Marius and done a flit!"

"Where could he do a flit to? Gibraltar ain't but about one and a quarter square miles, all told."

"There's Spain."

"They got a war on. He could never get across the frontier."

"Difficult," agreed the chief thoughtfully. "Still, if he once got across, by jing, and got himself all mixed up in the confusion over there, they'd find it mighty hard to retake him."

Harry screwed up one eye against the smoke coiling up from the cigarette in the corner of his mouth.

"We're guessin', anyway. What about them two Americans—Miss Brook an' that young Westray? Why ain't they come aboard? If the major's done a flit, they can't have nothin' to do with it."

"I dunno so much," said the chief. "Tell you for why. How's it been ever since they come aboard? It's been like this: Miss Brook's been interested in the major; you might say she's been chasin' after him, almost. And that young Westray, he's been interested in Miss Brook—chasin' after her, you might say. Looks to me as though there's somethin' screwy somewhere."

"What they call a 'plot'?" said Harry. "With somehow them four—Miss Brook and Westray, and Marius and the major—all mixed up together some way!" He inhaled deeply. "Last port of call, an' all, an' you reckoned the major's number was up, an' nothin' on earth could save him from arrivin' home to face his trial. Well, I tell you this, Bert. I can't help it, I never did like that

38

red-faced copper. If the major's done a flit, a sight I'd be sad to see is Marius bringin' him aboard with the bracelets on him. If he's done a flit, I hope he gets away with it!"

He leaned forward to look out of the open porthole. There across the sparkling water was the harbour wall, with the boom across the entrance; farther back, beyond the moored tugs and the two destroyers, were the galvanised iron sheds and the derricks; and behind the sheds, the town, trembled over by the heat-blur, climbed in a huddle of multi-coloured houses, with washing hung out on their flat roofs, to the beginning of the bare, towering Upper Rock with its camouflaged anti-aircraft and heavy gun emplacements. Right up on the ridged spine of the Rock, a heliograph was flashing from the signal station.

"Gib!" said Harry, the barman. "One and a quarter square miles!"

"That's the point," said the chief steward. "Last place on earth for a man to hide, an' get away with it! They know every mouse by its middle name on that Rock. If the major's done a flit, I bet a bottle of Hollands that he'll be sailin' for home along with us, all the same—in irons!"

"Get out o' my cabin," said Harry. "You croak like a bull frog!"

But, even though he was solid for the major, Harry, the barman, did not take that bet. It was too much like betting against a sure thing—as Inspector Sacarello of the Gibraltar police would have agreed.

Nothing resembling a murder case had happened on the Rock for years. The last had been open and shut. A Gibraltarian had thrown an elderly female relative from the flat roof of his house five stories to the street—with understandably fatal results. The excitement had come when the man was sentenced to death. There had been something resembling a riot when sentence was passed, for not in living memory had a native of the Rock been hanged by the neck. The civil population had made every effort to get a reprieve, but without success.

The murderer had hanged in the yard of the little

39

prison up under the ancient Moorish tower, where sometimes you can see the famous apes of Gibraltar. ("When the apes of Gibraltar die out," says the Spanish proverb, "the British will vanish from the Rock." The apes are pampered!)

For quite a time after that hanging, the Inspector had had his hands full; but that was old stuff now. Gibraltar was law-abiding. As a free port, it was the jumping-off place of a large contraband traffic with Spain, in tobacco and sugar; but the men engaged in it were mostly Spaniards, and the laws broken were mostly Spanish laws.

Run-of-the-mill routine filled the inspector's days—the enforcement of the motor and liquor licence laws; the surveillance of undesirable aliens; traffic control. His busiest times were when there was a fleet in—the Mediterranean Fleet or the Atlantic Fleet, or sometimes both; or when a U.S.A., German, French, or Greek squadron was visiting. Then the cabarets on Main Street hummed; the beer flowed like water; the rattle of castanets, the jangle of pianos, the squeak of fiddles went on all day—until eleven p.m. Eleven p.m. was closing-time, and it was Inspector Sacarello's business to see that it was observed.

It always was. Trust the inspector!

Right then—after eleven p.m.—was when the fur flew. Crowds of sailors, fresh from weeks at sea, emerged—full of beer, song, and the joys of spring—upon Main Street in the balmy semi-tropic night. They were ripe for mischief. They rode twelve to a taxi, roaring "Good Night, Sweetheart," catcalling, and whooping it up; and if they didn't like the taxi-driver's face, they were as likely as not to take his vehicle to pieces, section by section. All good, clean fun, high spirits, and no offence meant; but the inspector and his "bobbies"—as well as the Naval pickets and the redcaps—had their hands full when the fleets were in.

July 19th, 1936, changed all that for the inspector. On July 19th, 1936, General Francisco Franco proclaimed the revolt of the Spanish Army. All Spain went up in a sheet of flame, and Gibraltar was suddenly descended upon by hordes of refugees, numerous as locusts, and as hungry.

Life was changed for Inspector Sacarello. A thousand problems—commissariat, camping-space, billeting—beset him. The health graph dipped. The petty larceny graph took a sharp rise. Gibraltar's one small prison was of a sudden hopelessly inadequate.

The atmosphere was changed, too. A powder magazine makes an uneasy neighbour, and Spain was a powder magazine. The hot breath of war blew over neutral Gibraltar. There were "accidents". Shells from Spanish Government and Spanish insurgent battleships fell upon the Rock. Embattled 'planes from Morocco flew over it. There was tension in the air. Plotters of both sides tried to use Gibraltar as headquarters; newspapermen, war correspondents of many nationalities, photographers and newsreel men operated with the Rock as a Base. Reinforcements arrived—cruisers and destroyers—to stand by for any hostile developments. The population was swollen to capacity.

All this meant hard, worrying unremitting labour for Inspector Horacio Sacarello.

As the tide of war swept north across Spain toward Madrid, and east toward Malaga, the pressure was a little relieved. The inspector had time to think again. And what he thought, as he sat in his office on the afternoon of the day—a day some weeks after the fall of Malaga—when the s.s. *Llandnno Chief* arrived at Gibraltar, was this:

"They don't want a policeman in this job," the inspector thought. "They want a combined commissariat expert, diplomat, mathematician, distribution of population specialist, espionage and counter espionage sharp, a——"

That was as far as he got, for just then the telephone on his desk loosed a piercing jet of sound at him.

What he heard reacted upon him as though he had been stung by a hornet. He said only two words—"Touch nothing!"—hooked up that telephone, snatched the receiver from another.

This connected him with the police office at the Gibraltar gate. He gave rapid instructions, hung up, grabbed the receiver from a third telephone, connecting him with the Dock Police Office. More instructions.

Hooking up, he jammed down his thumb on a bell-push on his desk, then snatched a sheet of blue, official paper from a drawer, began to scribble.

The door opened. A very big, mountainously fat man, with a sergeant's stripes on his uniform, entered quickly, his helmet in his hand. Inspector Sacarello, writing rapidly, said:

"Murder! A stranger—apparently fresh off a ship. Dock Police say the only ship in today is the *Llandnno Chief*, homeward bound from Melbourne. I've had the dock gates closed, and the frontier gate. Here's an order"—he blotted it quickly—"to hold up the *Llandnno Chief*'s sailing. Run over to the Colonial Secretary's office with it, and the Supreme Court. Get the signatures, and serve it on the *Llandnno Chief*'s captain. Order my car as you go out—y pronto, hombre!"

Sergeant Mifsud saluted, vanished.

Seven minutes later—for there are no great distances in Gibraltar—Inspector Sacarello stepped from his neat, black Hillman Minx, and, leaving it entirely blocking the alley, pushed through the bead-curtained doorway into the Bar Monte Cristo.

The proprietor and the waiter were expecting him.

The little detective—for he was a small man, this Inspector Sacarello, dapper in white ducks, with a dusky, sharp face, dark eyes, a tuft of beard under his lower lip— shook hands with the proprietor, said without preamble:

"Where do we find him?"

The proprietor—thick-set, bald, pock-marked, in a black alpaca coat, and white trousers swathed about with a black sash—held aside a bead curtain. The inspector walked into the room, followed by the police surgeon and a uniformed constable.

The inspector's eyes photographed the scene—the cool, dim room, the big, open window, the cane chairs, small tables, rush mats, the Moorish chandelier. He glanced at the body of the heavy man reclining in the chair to the right of the window.

"Who found him, Garcia?"

"Jose here, inspector," said the proprietor of the bar.

The inspector made a sign to the doctor, who stepped forward to the body, opening his black bag. The inspector looked at the waiter.

"Just so you found him, Jose?"

"Just so, senor."

"That handkerchief?"

"It was spread over his face. He slept, the other gentleman said. I was not to disturb him. He gave me this." The waiter produced a Bank of Gibraltar one-pound note. "The other gentleman said he would return for his companion. He then left, senor.

"So, senor, after some time I look through curtain here. Gentleman still sleep. I enter to take away glass. By accident, I tread on gentleman's foot. He does not move. I tread hard, senor. It seem to me strange he does not move. I think he is ill. I draw away handkerchief from face. Blood! It is enough. I run from room, notify Senor Garcia."

"And this?" the inspector said sharply. He stooped, snatched up from the rush mat a thick, leather note-case, thrust it at Jose. "And this, hombre?"

The waiter shrugged, lying smoothly:

"No, see. I had not noticed it. A wallet, yes?"

"A wallet, Jose—for the bestowal of money," said the inspector, with bland irony. But his eyes had a gimlet keenness as they looked at the waiter. "Very well. We will leave this for the moment." He turned to the surgeon. "How go you?"

"There is little I can do here," said Dr. Azzopardi, and snapped shut his black case. "He is, of course, dead. It will be—cleaner, inspector, if I do not take out the stiletto until we have moved the body."

"Quite. And this stiletto?"

The inspector removed his white felt hat, tossed it on to

a table. Dr. Azzopardi had slightly changed the disposition of the body, so that the stiletto hilt was now visible, protruding from between the broad, blue shoulders.

The inspector stooped over the body, examining the stiletto hilt closely, but not touching it. The inspector's hair was black, parted in the centre, brushed up in two horns over the temples, and with a bald spot on top the size of a crown piece.

Garcia, the pock-marked owner of the bar, said:

"I should tell you, inspector, this is not the first time he has been here, this one."

"So?" The inspector's eyes were on the elephant-head hilt. "He is an old customer? On the telephone, you told me he was a stranger——"

"I do not know his name. But he has been here before —several times, always with a gap of some months between."

The inspector straightened, fingering the small tuft of hair under his lower lip.

"That is interesting, Garcia." He stood for a moment, frowning in thought, then turned again to the body, began systematically to go through the pockets. The contents—passport, papers, cigar-case, lighter, note-case, loose change, in a variety of currencies, and, surprisingly, a pair of handcuffs and an automatic—he placed in a neat pile on the low table.

Assuring himself that the pockets were now entirely emptied, he took up the passport. The photograph was that of the dead man; the full name given, James Chayne Marius; occupation, commercial traveller. With five years still to run before expiration, the visa pages were covered with rubber-stamp marks. During the past two years, James Chayne Marius, British subject by birth, had visited many countries, including recent visits to U.S.A. and Australia.

The inspector put down the passport, skimmed through the papers from the dead man's pockets. These papers were few, and impersonal—cards of hotels and business houses in various Eastern cities: such cards as any traveller has thrust upon him everywhere by dockside touts. There were no letters of any description, nor was there any pocket-book. But in the man's note-case, the inspector found, besides the equivalent in different currencies of some hundred and thirty-odd pounds, a card in a leather and mica frame.

The inspector stared at that card for a second in blank astonishment. It was a warrant card. It revealed James Chayne Marius, commercial traveller, to be, in fact, James Chayne Marius, Detective-Inspector, C.I.D., London. And a blue, official document in the note-case proved to be a warrant for the arrest of one Major Alan Bell-Evart.

Inspector Sacarello smiled thinly, his eyes gleaming. A native of Gibraltar, he had been educated in England. Police work was his passion. His knowledge of criminology was considerable. He had studied Scotland Yard methods, and Sûreté methods—and had worked his way to the top, in the police force of his native town, Gibraltar, without ever encountering a case that had made a real demand upon his knowledge or that had gained him space in English newspapers.

This case was different. It was going to make a splash. A Scotland Yard man, homeward bound with a prisoner, had been murdered by that prisoner—who else could the dead man's companion have been?—and Inspector Sacarello, of Gibraltar, was in charge of the case! Now, at last, England was going to hear of Inspector Sacarello.

He turned suddenly on the waiter.

"The dead man's companion, Jose—the man who gave you that pound note——"

"Si, senor?"

"Describe him."

The waiter did so.

Fifteen minutes later that description of Major Alan Bell-Evart went out from Gibraltar Radio Station.

Most houses, barber-shops, and cafes on the Rock subscribe to a radio service, whereby they are wired with

45

a rented loudspeaker. They have no set, just the loud-speaker, through which they receive programmes relayed from abroad, interspersed with local news bulletins and advertising announcements.

The Cafe Universal, just opposite the Hindu store of Chundra, Khitagara & Co., in Main Street, subscribed to the radio service.

With a tourist ship in, and two destroyers berthed in the harbour, this was a busy day for the Universal. The band, eight English girls brought out here on contract, had been playing indefatigably since noon; so, with half-hourly intervals, had the cabaret turns.

An interval had arrived. The band was taking an "easy" on its dais, over a cup of tea and a cigarette. The square of tiled floor where the cabaret performed was empty. The tables all about were crowded with tourists and sailors, with a scattering of Gibraltarians. Over the buzz of conversation rose the hollow booming of the loudspeaker.

"——Yorkshire, 284 for 7. Leyland, not out, 62. Those are the four o'clock scores. At the Theatre Royal tonight, Ronald Colman in 'A Tale of Two Cities'. Also full supporting programme. Here is a police announcement. We are asked by Inspector Sacarello to broadcast the following description of Major Alan Bell-Evart——"

A man who sat at a table near the window, looking across Main Street towards the store of Chundra, Khitagara & Co., turned his head suddenly, listening.

"——passenger aboard the s.s. *Llandnno Chief*," boomed the loudspeaker, "with whom the police are anxious to obtain an interview. Here is the description: Height, six feet; lean, athletic build; regular features, deeply sun-burned; clipped, black moustache; eyes, blue. Is wearing a white duck suit and panama. Any person having information as to the whereabouts of Major Alan Bell-Evart should communicate with Inspector Sacarello.

"Spanish news, General Quiepo de Llano, broadcasting last night from Radio Seville, declared——"

The man at the table near the window ceased to listen.

46

He glanced again across the sun-smitten, crowded Main Street at the rug-hung doorway of Chundra's, opposite. He was a young man of slender build, in a light grey, double-breasted suit. His face was clean-shaven, lean, brown, with a look of faintly ironical good humour. His hair was blond, parted at the side, brushed back smoothly, and a single eyeglass dangled on a black cord against his coat. His eyes were grey. They turned from their scrutiny of Chundra's to glance at the people at the tables each side of him.

At one table sat a group of Royal Engineer privates, in light khaki drill, with pipe-clayed belts and big, white pith helmets. At the other table were some sailors, white uniformed. All were intent on their own conversation.

The lean young man with the eyeglass put a hand in his breast pocket, drew out two British passports. He opened one, glancing at the photograph. The face was that of the man who, aboard the s.s. *Llandnno Chief*, had been known as Major Bell-Evart. But the name on the cover of the passport was A. J. Raffles.

The lean young man opened the second passport. His own face looked back at him. The name on the cover was B. J. S. Manders.

He sat for some moments with the passports in his hand, frowning at them—then glanced across again at Chundra's. A very tall, loose-limbed young man was in the act of emerging from the Hindu store.

The man called Manders thrust the two passports suddenly into his pocket, tossed a half-crown on the table beside his glass and, rising, walked quickly out of the Cafe Universal.

CHAPTER 5

SUNSET GUN

B. J. S. Manders—more familiarly, to his friend and partner, A. J. Raffles, "Bunny" Manders. Well known at Lord's, these two. Cricket in the summer, squash rackets in the winter.

Raffles was the better known—A. J. Raffles, of Abbeyshire, and a dozen M.C.C. and I.Z. tours; the same Raffles who topped the batting averages on the last West Indies tour, mainly because of a not out double century at Bridgetown, Barbados.

Only a man with a four-figure private income could afford to play, as an amateur, as much cricket as Raffles had played. And Raffles had a four-figure income. A private one. So private that there were not more than, perhaps, five people alive who knew he was a cracksman!

Raffles' passport, in Bunny Manders' pocket, described Raffles' occupation as "Independent". He was certainly that. Bunny Manders' own passport described Bunny as a "Journalist". And that is a description which covers a multitude of sins.

It was true, though, the excuse Bunny had given his partner, early in the year for not accompanying him to America. Bunny had said that he was writing a book. And it was a fact. He was. He had had that weak-minded ambition, that itch to write, long before he had thrown in his lot with Raffles. Every now and then it cropped out, and Bunny shut himself away and wrote a book.

He was writing one when Raffles took this idea into his head to visit the United States. He said it was "just to look round", but Bunny knew his partner. Something usually came of it when Raffles took a "look round". But Bunny stuck to his guns. America, he insisted, was not for him; he was going to finish his book or bust.

But he went up to Glasgow—wondering why Raffles should have chosen to travel by an obscure Glasgow-Montreal line—to see his friend off.

It was not until they were having a last drink in Raffles' cabin, while the stewards went round shouting "All those for the shore", that the debonair A. J. showed Bunny his passport. It was a nice new passport, in the name of "Alan Bell-Evart, Major".

How he had obtained it, he would not say. "A trade secret, old boy!" As to why he was choosing to travel on a false passport, he was equally reticent. "If it comes off, you'll know. If not, not."

He would not say what it was that might or might not "come off"—and Bunny, whose motto was "Faithful Unto Death", was tempted to stay aboard and go with his unscrupulous friend.

Raffles scotched that idea.

"Go home and write your book. You wanted it that way, you shall have it that way."

"Home", to the partners, comprised their chambers in the Albany. Bunny settled down there to his writing From time to time, cheery letters arrived from Raffles, in New York. He stayed there for some weeks, then moved to Philadelphia, and then—rather suddenly, it seemed to Bunny—right out west to San Francisco.

Bunny had one letter from San Francisco, then a card from Honolulu—a view of Waikiki Beach that made his mouth water.

That was the last he heard of Raffles for seven weeks.

He was pretty worried by the time the next letter arrived. It was from Melbourne, and it was dynamite.

Raffles was under arrest!

"A fair cop," Raffles wrote—"pinched on the cricket ground, while innocently watching Stan McCabe hooking 'em off his nose, past square leg. And pinched, oddly enough, by an English busy, on an English warrant, for a U.S. job! Never mind the details—no time for 'em. I've got just about three minutes to write this, and I'm hoping to bribe the bellhop of the hotel where I'm held to smuggle it out and post it. A detective-inspector of the name of Marius is my ball-and-chain, and the warrant is for 'Bell-Evart'. He's no idea it's an alias. I understand he's bringing me home to durance vile on the s.s. *Llandnno Chief.* I'm gummed up all right, this time; ten years is the maximum, and no lawyer living, I'm afraid, is going to honey-tongue me out with less. As for you, my advice is: Get out, change your name, vanish! There's no saying what may come out in the wash——"

Raffles was right there. The first thing that, sooner or later, was bound to come out was the true identity of "Major Alan Bell-Evart". That would mean a police visit to the partners' Albany Chambers.

Bunny, with a sick feeling at the pit of his stomach, went through all the papers in the chambers with a small tooth-comb. Nothing in the slightest degree incriminating must be found here.

It was while on this job that Bunny came across Raffles' own passport. He pondered over this for some time, thinking hard; then looked up the shipping news in the paper. The *Llandnno Chief* was by now somewhere in the Red Sea.

Bunny went out and bought himself a ticket, P & O, to Gibraltar. He arrived there some days before the *Llandnno Chief* was due. They were wretched days for Bunny. "Ten years maximum," Raffles had said. Ten years! Old A. J., who enjoyed life to the hilt—who burgled a house in the same spirit as he played his cricket, taking the sporting chance every time. Old A. J., stitching mailbags behind bars for the ten best years of his life!

Not, Bunny swore, not if he knew it. He didn't know what he could do, quite. Once they got Raffles to England, it was all up, of course. That was why he had come to Gib. As long as Raffles was in transit, something might possibly be done. This extra passport, Raffles' own pass-port, was a definite asset. The problem was, how to get in touch with Raffles?

Bunny was down at the docks when the *Llandnno Chief* dropped her anchor in the sparkling bay, outside the boomed harbour. He saw the quarantine boat go out. He saw the first tender go out, take aboard its load, head for the shore. His plan was to go out with the tender when it returned to the ship. That Raffles would be allowed ashore was an idea that never entered his head.

His heart turned a complete handspring when he saw Raffles come down the gangway from the tender. He stepped back quickly into the shelter of the Bland Line shed. The big, red-faced merchant with Raffles was obviously Detective-Inspector Marius.

Bunny followed them up into the town, saw them enter the Bar Monte Cristo.

He hung about on the corner of Main Street, keeping watch on the alley, desperately anxious.

When he saw Raffles emerge alone from the bar, and turned down Main Street, Bunny could not believe his eyes. Where was Marius? There was something fishy somewhere.

He tried discreetly to attract Raffles' attention, and his partner looked straight at him across Main Street. He did not give a sign of recognition—and Bunny, not knowing what had happened in the Bar Monte Cristo, not realising Raffles' terrific preoccupation, not guessing that his friend had looked straight at him without in fact seeing him at all, took that blank stare as a signal to lie low.

At a discreet distance, Bunny followed Raffles down Main Street, saw him enter the Piccadilly Bar, saw him leave it, walk back up Main Street, enter Chundra's.

Bunny went into the Cafe Universal, opposite, chose a seat in the window, watched. Raffles, just inside the store, stood talking to a long, loose-limbed youngster with blond, untidy hair. Then he passed from view, somewhere into the back of the shop.

Bunny kept vigil there in the window of the Cafe Universal while the girls' orchestra went through a dozen numbers and the cabaret twice through its turns.

Raffles did not emerge from Chundra's.

Then, shocking Bunny's heart into his throat, came that radio announcement: "Major Bell-Evart—wanted——"

A minute later, that loose-limbed youngster, to whom he had seen Raffles talking, emerged from Chundra's and turned down Main Street—and Bunny was after him like a hare.

He caught him up before he had walked ten paces from Chundra's.

"Just a moment——"

Dan Westray stopped, turned. He was taller than the slightly-built, elegant Bunny.

"Don't think this cheek," Bunny said. "Some time ago I saw a man I believe I know go into that Hindu store up there. I wasn't quite sure, and I've been waiting for him to come out, to get another look at him. But confound it, he hasn't come out!"

"So what?"

Bunny grinned.

"I'd look a fool if I hung about any longer, and he turned out not to be the man I think he is. I saw him talking to you when he first went in. You seemed to know each other. I wonder if you could tell me his name?"

"Sure—Bell-Evart," said Dan Westray; "Major Alan Bell-Evart. Off the *Llandnno Chief*, both of us." He stared at Bunny reflectively, his eyes blue-grey—then nodded slowly. "That's right, by golly—he hasn't come out, has he? That makes two of 'em——"

"I don't quite follow," Bunny said courteously.

He was thinking fast. The radio had announced that Raffles, alias Bell-Evart, was wanted. Raffles was in Chundra's. He was alone there. The burning hope in Bunny's mind was that Raffles had shaken off Marius, that he had some friend in Chundra's, that Chundra's was a bolt-hole. If that were so, this loose-limbed young man was a menace. He knew where Raffles was. The moment he heard of the radio announcement, he would notify the police, send them hotfoot to Chundra's. It was to prevent that that Bunny had buttonholed this lean, long young man. Somehow, he must stall him; he must see that he did not get wind of that radio announcement.

"You don't follow, eh?" Dan Westray said. He hesitated, added abruptly: "Is Bell-Evart the man you thought? Is he a friend of yours?"

"You might," Bunny said cautiously, "call him that."

"Then we're in the same boat," said Dan Westray— "you and me both. We ought to get together." He glanced about him. "How about that joint over there?"

The "joint" indicated was the Cafe Universal, from which Bunny had just come. They returned to it together, took the window-table at which Bunny had sat before. The piano was jangling "La Prisionera"; a flashing-eyed, dark girl in Mexican hat and trousers was dancing a Sevillana, her red heels clattering on the tiled floor-space in the centre of the room, her castanets rattling.

The customers now were mostly soldiers, sailors and Gibraltarians. The majority of the tourists were gone.

Dan Westray lighted a cigarette.

"You're puzzled about your friend, Bell-Evart," he said. "I'm worried about a young lady—a Miss Drusilla Brook. She went into that joint before Bell-Evart did, and she hasn't come out yet, either. I waited as long as I could, then I tackled a fat Hindu in there who seemed to be the boss salesman. I asked him to go in and tell the young lady that I—Dan Westray's my name—was waiting for her."

"Yes?" Bunny said.

"He looked at me," said Dan Westray, "as though I'd got a touch of the sun. He said that as far as he knew, no young lady had gone through into the back rooms. I described her. He said he had no recollection of ever having seen any such party, but he'd have a look for me. I said, 'O.K., I'll come with you.'

"He didn't object. There are a couple of rooms, full of junk, out at the back of the store. He said she must be in one of them, if she was there at all. Well"—Dan Westray drew deeply on his cigarette—"she wasn't!"

"Is there a back way out?" Bunny asked.

"There's a side door that opens from one of the rooms on to an alley. The Hindu pointed it out to me—said she might have left that way, if she'd ever been in there at all. But he made it pretty clear that he thought I was mistaken in believing she'd ever entered the place."

"No chance that you were—mistaken?"

"Not a chance!" Dan Westray said violently. "I tell you she went into that joint, and so—a bit later—did Bell-Evart. And you've been watching for Bell-Evart, and I've been watching for Drusilla—and neither of 'em have come out, at any rate, through the store. I don't know what you think, but I tell you frankly, I think the show that fat Hindu put on of never having seen Drusilla is as screwy as all Hades!"

He looked at Bunny keenly.

"I don't know how well you know Bell-Evart. Me, I joined the *Llandnno Chief* at Port Said; I spoke to Miss Brook and Bell-Evart for the first time in the tender there, going out to the ship. Miss Brook, like me, was joining her there; Bell-Evart, and an inseparable sidekick of his called Marius, had been ashore looking around. Miss Brook had never seen Bell-Evart before in her life, but for some reason or other she was mighty interested in him from the moment she met him."

Bunny sipped his coffee.

"What are you suggesting—that they had some arrangement to rendezvous over there in Chundra's?"

"On the level, I don't know what to think," Dan Westray said worriedly. "They went into Chundra's, and through to the back of the shop—first Drusilla, and then, a bit later, Bell-Evart. All I know is, that they haven't come out."

Bunny polished his eyeglass abstractedly, staring across Main Street at the enigmatic establishment of Chundra, Khitagara & Co. He said abruptly:

"Where were you headed when I saw you?"

"Back to the ship. There's just a chance, of course, that she may have left by that side entrance."

"And if—" Bunny said gently, "if you hadn't found her on board? What were you planning to do then?"

As he spoke, there was a surge of handclapping. The

54

piano ceased, the dancer bowed herself off the floor, the radio blared on suddenly, in mid-sentence:

"——request of Inspector Sacarello. Here, again, is a description of Major Alan Bell-Evart, with whom the police are anxious to obtain an interview. Height——"

Dan Westray half rose, staring at Bunny—then sank back slowly into his chair. The radio boomed out its description of Major Bell-Evart, went on to announce a programme of gramophone records. Dan Westray had not taken his eyes from Bunny Manders. Now the young American spoke, harshly:

"What's the meaning of that?"

Bunny lighted a cigarette. His heart beat violently The last thing he had wanted was for Westray to hear that broadcast. He had not dreamed that it would be repeated so soon. But the damage was done now, and for the life of him he could not see what he could do about it. He shrugged.

"Search me. Evidently the major's wanted. You and I know where he is—or where he very recently was. I'm a friend of his; I, naturally, am not going to tell the police where I saw the major last. As far as I'm concerned, let 'em get on with it. You're differently placed. It's up to you, I suppose, to go and tell the police you believe the major to be in Chundra's."

Dan Westray looked across at the Hindu store, then back at Bunny.

"Listen," he said. "You don't want the police to find your friend, Bell-Evart. O.K., I'll tell you something. I want to locate Miss Brook. I've got to locate her. But I've a mighty good reason for not calling in any police help on the job!"

Bunny exhaled a long breath. Every nerve in his body seemed to relax. He said:

"Westray, you've taken a ton-weight off my mind. I'll tell you something now. Bell-Evart"—he had no intention of revealing Raffles' real name—"has been a prisoner aboard that ship. He's been under arrest, en route to trial. Marius is a Scotland Yard man. What Bell-Evart's charged with, I don't know; but from that radio announcement, I'm guessing that the major's skipped Marius and is on the run. And I want him to get away, Westray, that's all I'm interested in, I want him to make the skip. There you are. My cards are on the table. I don't want you to incriminate yourself, or get mixed up in Bell-Evart's attempt to break arrest. I'm not asking you for help; I'm offering it. Keep quiet about where you saw Bell-Evart last, and I'll help you every way I can to locate Miss Brook. How's that?"

"Sold," said Dan. "It's a deal. And we'll get busy right now. The first thing is to find out if she has, by any chance, returned to the ship——"

As the two men left the Cafe Universal, a pedlar who had been circulating among the tables with a napkin-covered basket containing crayfish—"gorda, fresca, muy buena!"—quite suddenly abandoned his peddling, and moved towards the door. Neither Bunny Manders nor Dan Westray noticed him.

They hired a gharry to the docks. As they passed under the old bridge called the Water Gate, a neat little black Hillman Minx hummed by, going in the opposite direction.

Inspector Sacarello's car, though Manders and Westray didn't know that.

Their gharry clip-clopped on down to the docks. The light was fading now into the brief Southern dusk. The wide bay was aflame with sunset; the gaunt hills behind the white town of Algeciras, far across the bay, stood dark against the fire in the sky behind them. The sunset gun boomed from the Rock, there was a cry of bugles, the colours on the two destroyers in the Inner Harbour came fluttering down.

"Lord," Dan Westray exclaimed suddenly, "the last tender from the shore was four-thirty! I haven't given it a thought. It's after six now."

Bunny, ducking out from the gharry, said:

"Don't worry. The old hooker's still there."

The *Llandnno Chief*, showing no immediate signs of

departure, lay at anchor outside the boomed harbour. A white ship on that blood-red water, already she was challenging the sunset with a few pale, twinkling lights.

"Maybe," Dan said, "but how do we get out to her?"

"I take it you don't want to get out to her, anyway, unless Miss Brook's aboard? And if she's aboard," said Bunny, "they'll have checked her passport at the office there before she went on to the tender."

They crossed to the office, where Dan addressed the policeman who sat at a desk in the window.

"Brook?" said the policeman. "Step in, gentlemen."

To the left of the window, the door stood open. Dan stepped in, Bunny following. In a cane chair in the small, sparsely furnished office sat a swarthy, mountainously fat police-sergeant—Sergeant Mifsud—with a helmet on his knee. He nodded.

"Passengers from the *Llandnno Chief*, gentlemen?"

"I am," said Dan.

The sergeant looked at Bunny.

"And you, sir?"

"No," said Bunny. "I'm staying in Gibraltar. Peak Hotel."

The sergeant addressed Dan again:

"You know the last tender for the ship left some time ago?"

"Yes," Dan said. "I——"

The constable at the window-desk, who had been running a thick forefinger down a foolscap list of names and numbers, now turned.

"Miss Brook's passport is checked out of the docks, but not in. The lady's still ashore."

Bunny and Dan exchanged a quick glance.

"Thanks very much," Dan said, and turned to the door.

It slammed in his face, kicked shut by a large, square-toed boot. Sergeant Mifsud rose mountainously from his chair.

"Not so fast, gentlemen," he said smoothly—"not so fast!"

CHAPTER 6

THE DEAD KNOCK ONCE

INSPECTOR Sacarello's neat Hillman Minx, when it passed Bunny Manders and Dan Westray under the Water Gate, was on its way back to police headquarters.

The inspector was not letting the grass grow under his feet. He had just, at the time he passed Bunny and Dan, come from the *Llandnno Chief*. He had interviewed the captain, who had told him how Marius and Bell-Evart had come aboard at Melbourne.

Marius, it seemed, had gone immediately and privately to the captain, produced his warrant, explained the position.

"He suggested," the captain told Inspector Sacarello, "that for the general peace of mind of the passengers, Bell-Evart should be treated as an ordinary passenger. I was glad enough to agree; I had nothing against the man; I was sorry for him. Marius, of course, took full responsibility."

The last shore tender had already brought out its passengers. Four were missing—Marius, Bell-Evart, Dan Westray, Jr., and a Miss Drusilla Brook.

"Now, about these last two," said the inspector. "As they weren't here on time, would you in normal circumstances have sailed without them?"

"I certainly should. Cards giving sailing times and so on are put in each passenger's cabin the night before we enter a port. My crew has other things to do than run around after stray passengers!"

Inspector Sacarello went up to the Marconi cabin, where he learned that throughout the voyage no messages of any kind had been sent either by Detective-Inspector Marius or Major Alan Bell-Evart. He then went down to A deck. Here the Scotland Yard man and his prisoner had shared a cabin.

The inspector went through the cabin carefully, and through the effects of both men. He then had them packed to take ashore with him.

The little detective was enjoying himself. This case was open-and-shut. Bell-Evart was the murderer. He was somewhere in Gibraltar, and every exit was barred to him. He hadn't one chance in a thousand of getting out. Even now, as the inspector's Hillman Minx with his favourite constable at the wheel, slid up Main Street, the radio was blasting out Bell-Evart's description every fifteen minutes. Scotland Yard had been notified by cable of the murder of its operative; no doubt, there would be a reply awaiting the inspector on his desk.

Already he had given an interview to the editor of the *Gibraltar Chronicle*, who was also the correspondent of a big London news agency. By this time tomorrow the name of Sacarello would be on the map; the London correspondents and photographers, of whom Gib was full at the moment, owing to the fighting in Spain, would be shortly besieging him. Perhaps even a newsreel man——

The inspector lighted a short, black cigar. He felt on top of the world. Bell-Evart couldn't possibly remain long at large. The inspector almost hoped the fugitive would do something spectacular—put up a fight, for example, when they closed in on him. "Scotland Yard Man Murdered; Inspector Sacarello Corners Killer!"

The newshawks had got wind of the *Llandnno Chief*'s delayed sailing, and the Bell-Evart radio call, even quicker than the inspector had thought likely. The charge-room at headquarters was full of them—correspondents down from the Madrid and Guadalajara fronts to send home uncensored war reports from British territory.

Inspector Sacarello stalked through them importantly, waving his cigar.

"Later! Later!"

This affair, he thought, as he entered his own office, could hardly have broken prettier for him. At what other time would Gib have been swarming like this with top-flight newshawks?

A "Via Imperial" cable lay on his desk. The reply from the Yard! He tore it open, sat down in the desk-chair with the unshaded electric light shining on his crown-piece bald spot, took his code-book from a locked drawer, went to work swiftly.

In three minutes the decoded message lay complete before him.

He read it through.

His jaw slowly sagged, the cigar fell from his mouth, he sprang suddenly to his feet. Rigid, incredulous, he read through the decoded message a second time:

YOUR CABLE RECEIVED. THERE IS NO SUCH PERSON AS DETECTIVE-INSPECTOR MARIUS. JAMES CHAYNE MARIUS, BRITISH SUBJECT BY BIRTH, DESCRIBED AS COMMERCIAL TRAVELLER, IS IN PASSPORT OFFICE RECORDS. IF CLAIMING POSITION DETECTIVE-INSPECTOR C.I.D., IS IMPOSTER. NAME OF BELL-EVART IS UNKNOWN BOTH IN OUR RECORDS AND THOSE OF PASSPORT OFFICE. IF HE HOLDS PASSPORT IN THIS NAME, IT IS FORGED. RE WARRANT IN MARIUS' POSSESSION, NO WARRANT HAS EVER BEEN ISSUED HERE FOR ARREST OF BELL-EVART. HENCE THIS, TOO, MUST BE FORGED. KINDLY ADVISE US DEVELOPMENTS.

Inspector Sacarello dropped back into his desk-chair as though his knees had gone weak under him. He sat staring at the cable. His face was like a triangle of yellow parchment.

The dead man, Marius, a fake—not a Yardman at all? Impossible!

From a drawer of his desk, he snatched Marius' warrant-card, examined it closely. It was perfect; every detail was correct. A forgery? The inspector could not believe it!

From the same drawer he took Marius' warrant for the arrest of Alan Bell-Evart. In the warrant, too, every detail was correct. He held up the blue paper to the light. Even the water-mark was authentic. It was official paper.

The inspector lighted a fresh cigar. One thing only about that warrant struck him as queer. Bell-Evart was to be arrested, according to the warrant, for robbery with violence at the residence of Mr. Andrew Payne Hulburd, Forge Park, Westchester County, N.Y., U.S.A. An American job! Why, then, a Scotland Yard warrant?

The inspector smoked furiously.

Impossible to believe that Scotland Yard was mistaken —that Marius was their man, that he was using the name of Marius as an alias to aid him in his official business, and that the Yard was uninformed of the alias. No, no; impossible, that! For the simple reason that the Yard denied all knowledge of the issuance of the warrant and of the existence of Bell-Evart!

It was incredible. It was revolutionary. Yet it must be true!

Marius had "arrested" Bell-Evart in Melbourne. He had brought him as far as Gibraltar, on the *Llandnno Chief*, as a prisoner. The captain of the ship had not doubted his bona fides. (The inspector made a note to cable Melbourne. Perhaps Marius had at no time communicated with the police there. He, the inspector, would find out.) No single person with whom he had come in contact seemed to have doubted Marius' bona fides.

How about the prisoner himself? Bell-Evart, so-called. Had he believed Marius to be the Yard man he pretended, or had he known him to be a fake? Impossible to guess.

One thing he could do—he made another note—was to cable Westchester County. Had there actually been a robbery, with violence, at Forge Park in the night in question? Or was the charge against Bell-Evart as fake as the warrant itself?

That, at least, Inspector Sacarello told himself, was one point he could check. And then he must tighten every strand of the drag-net he had out for Bell-Evart.

Impostor Marius might be, but he was dead—murdered, and the man who called himself Bell-Evart had killed him.

What had seemed an open-and-shut case had in a flash been shattered by the cable from Scotland Yard. It was no longer straightforward. It was mysterious and unique. Who was this James Chayne Marius? Why had he posed as a Yard man? Why had he "arrested" Bell-Evart? Where was he taking him? Who was Bell-Evart himself?

The case was bigger than Inspector Sacarello had ever dreamed. But one fact remained constant. Bell-Evart had killed Marius. Bell-Evart was at large, and must be taken, and quickly.

Decisively, the little inspector jammed his cigar into a corner of his mouth, lifted a small, black attache-case on to his desk, began to pack into it the various papers and exhibits relating to the case. There was, first, the stiletto with ivory elephant-head hilt, which he had now received from Dr. Azzopardi. There was the photograph of a fingerprint found on the hilt of the weapon. There was the Yard cable. In addition, there were Marius' fake warrant card, his fake warrant, and the various contents of his pockets.

The inspector packed these, locked the case, and five minutes later, in his black Hillman Minx, having dismissed his constable-chauffeur, he was humming through the blossom-filled gardens of the Alameda.

The little man had, among the British officers of the garrison, a friend, one Captain Kerry Adam, M.C. Captain Adam was, nominally, a soldier. Actually, his work more closely resembled that of a detective. He was in charge of intelligence on the Rock. He was a military sleuth. His knowledge of criminology—the common interest which had brought about his friendship with the inspector—was greater than his knowledge of military tactics and strategy.

The Marius' case did not come within Captain Kerry Adam's province. It was entirely Inspector Sacarello's affair. Nevertheless, the inspector felt the need to hear his friend's views of the case. That was why he had brought with him the various exhibits. Captain Adam was an acute man, the inspector's good friend, and utterly without professional jealousy.

The officers' quarters are scattered here and there about the Rock. The pleasantest of them are out at the most southerly point—Europa Point. Here, one of a row of attractive white bungalows along the top of a low cliff, was Captain Adam's menage.

The inspector swung his car into this side road. It was very short, a cul-de-sac, sloping upward. A high, white wall, picked out with green doors—each of which had painted upon it the name and regiment of an officer—ran the length of the cul-de-sac, on the left. On the right was the cliff-edge, guarded by a two-foot-high concrete kerb. You could hear the uneasy sea snoring in the rocks at the foot of the cliff; out beyond, the sea stretched, vaguely glimmering, far into the night; and there, over the mountains of Africa, over the Jebel Musa, the moon was now rising.

The headlights of the Hillman shone blankly white on the wall to the left; here and there the feathery head of a date palm, leaning over the wall, cast a blur of purple shadow.

Captain Adam's house was the last in the cul-de-sac. Inspector Sacarello drew up before it, snapped off his headlights. The sidelights remained, glimmering palely on the great buttress of rock which lay like a barrier across the cul-de-sac. The branches of an old, giant fig-tree, growing in the captain's garden, hung low over the wall. A radio was playing a foxtrot, somewhere close— probably on Captain Adam's veranda.

As the little inspector climbed out of his Hillman, took his black attache-case from the seat, the music ceased, and the voice of the Gibraltar announcer boomed forth:

"Here is a police announcement. We are requested by Inspector Sacarello to broadcast the following description of Major Alan Bell-Evart, passenger——"

The inspector, attache-case in hand, white felt hat drawn down over his eyes, cigar in a corner of his mouth, stood listening.

"Any person," concluded the announcement, "having information as to the whereabouts of Major Bell-Evart should communicate at once with Inspector Sacarello. Continuing our programme of gramophone records——"

The inspector shrugged one shoulder, and, as the music started again, crossed to the door in the wall. His hand was raised to the bell-push when a sound, a slight, swift shuffling in the dust, arrested his attention. He peered into the sable shadow of the fig-tree, and in the same second, before he could raise a finger to defend himself, a black shape launched at him, staggering him backward.

He stumbled, lost his balance, and, dropping the attache-case, threw out his hands behind him to arrest his fall.

With swift, silent savagery, the attacker hurled himself down upon the fallen man. Knees drove into the pit of the inspector's stomach, flattening him, striking the breath from his body. Before he could wrench free, hands—lean, steel-strong, murderous—crushed in on his throat.

Fiercely, mercilessly, the hands tightened——

The radio on Captain Kerry Adam's veranda, beyond the high, white wall, continued to waft out upon the quiet night the vibrant music of Albeniz's Tango. A voice called:

"Tucker! Tucker!"

"Sir?"

"Tune down that infernal radio! It's deafening, man!"

"Very good, sir."

The radio pee-eeped, pee-eeped once or twice, then was muted to a lower note. It was a portable set; it stood on a cane table on the low, mosquito-screened veranda. Light fell across the small garden, which was bounded in front by the high wall, to the right by another high wall, and to the left by the towering bastion of rock.

There were small, tiled paths in the garden, and beds of flaming azalea and other shrubs; here and there were clumps of the tall Spanish Bayonet cactus; there were one or two date palms, a dark, pointed cypress, and, over against the wall, the gnarled, enormous fig-tree.

Private Tucker, the captain's batman, took his hand from the tuning dial, turned to cast a glance over the larger table nearby, which was laid for dinner with three covers. Two electric, primrose-shaded, reading lamps stood on the table.

Private Tucker, short, bald, rubicund, in light khaki drill tunic and slacks satisfied himself that he had forgotten nothing in setting the table, and was about to re-enter the bungalow when the captain came out, shaking the folds from a handkerchief.

"Did you hear a car drive up a minute ago, Tucker?"

"I thought I did—yes, sir. It must have been someone for Major Rainbird, next door, sir. Sherry, sir?"

"All right, I'll help myself. You cut along and make sure that leg of lamb's not burning. And another time, don't tune up that radio so high. If you tune it up so that you can hear it in the kitchen, it deafens us out in front here. I've told you about that before. You must curb your passion for music, Tucker."

"Very good, sir."

Tucker clicked the heels of his heavy boots and marched stiff-backed into the house.

Decanters and glasses were on the small table beside the radio set. Captain Adam poured himself a glass of sherry. He was a bulky, pink-faced man, with yellow hair brushed straight back, a yellow, toothbrush moustache, and blue, shrewd, twinkling eyes. He wore a mess jacket. He stood sipping his sherry, and turned as a step sounded on the veranda. It was one of his guests.

The captain grinned.

"Hallo, Tinker! Sherry? It's all sherry here, you know. It's a crime to drink cocktails, with Jerez just over the Spanish border there. Pity this war's on, or I'd run you and Blake up to Jerez to see the sherry bodegas—Gonzales-Byass, Domecq, and the rest of 'em. Help yourself. There's Merito, Manzanilla, Solera, and half a dozen others."

"I don't know the first thing about it," said the young

man called Tinker, cheerfully; "they all look pretty good to me."

"Try the pale one," said Captain Adam. "That's Manzanilla. That's the real wine of Spain. Give any Spaniard a couple of bottles of that and it'd take a gag to stop him singing flamenco at you.

"Confound it," he went on, "I'm sick that you and your guv'nor should have turned up just when this beastly war is on. You gave me a good time when I was over in London on that rum business about the general with the wrong medals. I'd like to have given you a good time here, but there's nothing much in the way of diversion in Gib. We garrison folk get our fun across the frontier—up at La Cruz and Miraflores; and now this war's closed the frontier. All we can do is to run up to the garrison mess after dinner and play some billiards; there's damn all else."

Tinker grinned. He was a slender, tough-looking young man, with a keen brown face. He wore white flannels, and a blue, double-breasted coat.

"Don't worry about us. That British Legation case that brought us over to Tangier kept us pretty busy for three weeks. The guv'nor said, when he wound the case up day before yesterday, that as we had five days to wait for our boat home, he hoped we'd be able to spend them quietly—get a spot of rest. That's why he took you up on that old invitation of yours, and we caught the ferry over from Tangier to park ourselves on you."

"You'll get plenty of rest, all right," said the captain, and added: "Ah, here's your guv'nor at last! Good! Another two minutes, Blake, and I couldn't have taken responsibility for that leg of lamb Tucker's got in the oven. His front name's Alfred, and he'd burn the cakes as soon as look. Sherry?"

He waved a hand at the side table, and Blake helped himself to a glass of Manzanilla.

"Nothing," he asked, as he replaced the stopper in the decanter, "from your little inspector friend?"

"Not a word," said Captain Adam, "but don't worry,

he'll be along sooner or later. Any case a bit out of the ordinary he always comes along and talks over with me. He's a likeable little chap, Horacio Sacarello, and he knows his stuff. There's not much scope here in Gib, but he'll be heard of one day. When I introduce him to you—Blake, the criminologist, in person—he'll be all over you. He'll talk a tin ear on to you with his questions."

Blake smiled. Spare and tall, he wore, like his assistant, Tinker, white flannels and a blue, double-breasted coat. His keen, clean-shaven, aquiline face was deeply tanned—a desert tan. (Only a week before, acting for the British Legation in Tangier, he had been riding—burnoused like a Bedouin Arab—with a squadron of Moorish regulares in the desert foothills of El Rif.) His eyes were grey and deep-set; his dark, crisp hair was deeply receded above the temples. But his smile was easy and pleasant.

"I'm looking forward to meeting your little inspector. I'm interested in that radio call he's been putting out."

"Any ideas about it?" his host asked.

Private Tucker came out on to the veranda with the hors d'œuvres at that moment, and the three took their places at the table before Blake answered:

"None. How could I have? We don't know anything about what's behind it. But I'm rather interested, because the description, as broadcast, of this Major Alan Bell-Evart, is identical with that of a man we once crossed swords with. Eh, Tinker?"

Tinker grinned, spearing an anchovy with his fork.

"The Fetter of Buddha. Somerset."

"Precisely," Blake said, in a dry tone.

"All this is very cryptic," said Captain Adam.

"I want to meet your little inspector," Blake said. "I want to hear more about this Bell-Evart. If he turns out to be the man I'm thinking of, I'll tell you what I know about him."

Almost as he spoke, the radio, which had been playing, stopped, and Captain Adam was on the point of speaking when a clear, loud knock sounded on the door in the wall.

"Blast," said the captain. "Tucker's dishing up, and I

wouldn't have that leg o' lamb spoiled for worlds. Excuse me——"

He tossed his napkin on to the table, opened the screen-door of the veranda, walked down the tiled path to the door in the wall.

Both Blake and Tinker saw him open the door, saw a figure in white ducks pitch forward into his arms, heard his sudden, startled shout.

Blake was up in an instant, striding down the path.

"What's wrong?"

Captain Adam was lowering the figure gently on to the tiles. It was that of a small, spare, dark-skinned man with a tuft of beard under his lower lip and a bald spot the size of a crown-piece on top of his head. The face was terribly suffused, the eyes staring, the tongue protruding.

Captain Adam put an ear to the man's chest, felt the pulse in the wrist, then rose slowly.

"Dead!" He looked at Blake grimly. "Strangled!"

"The little inspector?"

Captain Adam nodded.

Blake stepped quickly through the doorway.

The dusty road was empty, save for the Hillman Minx.

CHAPTER 7

YELLOW HALF-MOONS

INSPECTOR Sacarello's radio description of Major Alan Bell-Evart, so-called, had arrested the attention of Blake, the criminologist, by its resemblance to that of a man with whom, as he had put it to Tinker, he had once "crossed swords".

That same radio description arrested the attention of A. J. Raffles himself, alias Bell-Evart, by its accuracy.

Following his singular interview with the fat Hindu in the back room of Messrs. Chundra, Khitagara & Co.'s store; following the moment when he had seen the waiter in the Bar Monte Cristo, across the alley, attempt to rob the dead body of Detective-Inspector Marius; following the fat Hindu's hissed warning, as he drew the shutters closed: "Within twenty minutes, the fortress of Gibraltar will be mobilised for your capture, Major Alan Bell-Evart —or should I say Mr. A. J. Raffles?"—following these events, Raffles had accompanied the Hindu up a flight of dark stairs to a room on the first floor, over the shop.

"You wait here, please," the Hindu said, in his curious, allusive, babu English. "Presentlee my employer will see you—Mr. Nanda Lal Chundra. Here you will be safe— oah, yes."

He smiled with a flash of white teeth in his dusky, moon face and, stepping quickly backward, drew the door to after him. A large prayer-rug swayed into place across the door; and when Raffles twitched the rug aside, it was to see that the door, closely fitting in the wall, had on the inside neither keyhole nor handle.

With a shrug, a slight, grim smile, the adventurer let the prayer-rug fall back into place. He was, it appeared, trapped. That was one aspect of the situation. The other was, that so long as he was trapped in Chundra's, he was out of the hands of the police.

There were few cooler men in a jam than A. J. Raffles. He took out his cigarette-case and, tapping a cigarette on it, glanced round the room.

It was dim and hot. The shutters were closed; through the slats of them strips of sunlight fell across a cushioned divan in the window and across a section of the coconut-matting which covered the floor. The room was entirely Eastern. Pouffes dotted the floor, and low tables of ebony and ivory; the walls were hung with prayer-rugs; here and there, in niches and on small shelves, stood Turkish coffee-pots of brass and copper, and hubble-bubble pipes. There was a faint, steady buzz of flies in the dim, still, uncomfortably hot room.

Raffles lighted his cigarette and, snapping out his lighter, crossed to the window. He tossed his panama on to one of the low tables, peered out through the slats of the shutters. He could see little but the flat glare of the sun on the buildings opposite. He unlatched one of the shutters and drew it a trifle open, so that, himself unseen, he could look down obliquely upon the crowding, colourful traffic of Main Street.

He stood there smoking, watching the traffic—reflecting grimly that those white-clad people who went clip-clopping gaily past in the white-canopied horse-carriages, and honked busily by in the big, open American touring-cars, were for the most part his fellow-passengers from the *Llandnno Chief*.

He had never in his adventurous life been more strangely or precariously placed.

Sooner or later, presumably, Messrs. Chundra, Khita-gara & Co.'s motive for providing him with this sanctuary would be made plain. Till then——

Till then, he thought with a tightening of the lips, he was free to wonder just where the American girl, Drusilla Brook, fitted into this mystery. She had been in that back room a second before Marius' death in the room opposite, across the alley; a second after his death, she had vanished. Yet, an appreciable time later, Dan Westray had declared positively that Drusilla was still somewhere in the store!

Was she still here?

Raffles glanced across toward the prayer-rug that hid the door. He opened the shutter a trifle wider. The sill of the window was low to the floor; outside the window was a narrow, wrought-iron balcony.

He drew up a pouffe, sat down on it. The entrance to the store, being directly below him, was out of his line of vision; but he could see part of the crowded street, the opposite pavement, and the door of a cafe across there—Cafe Universal. Above the din of the traffic, there penetrated to him music from the cafe, the click of dancing heels, the rattle of castanets.

If Dan Westray had not already left the store, and if when he did leave it he crossed to the opposite side of the street, from here Raffles would be able to see him—and to see if Drusilla were with him.

Raffles sat smoking, keeping vigil for the entrance into this room of Nanda Lal Chundra, or Dan Westray's exit from the store below—whichever event might next occur.

But what occurred next was neither of these things.

So suddenly that it brought Raffles, with a shock, to his feet, a voice spoke quietly behind him.

He wheeled. The room was empty. In an instant, he realised that the voice was that of a radio loudspeaker. He located it almost at once, in a niche in the wall to his left; the loudspeaker must have been switched on from an adjoining room.

Stockstill, he listened to the broadcast of his own description. It struck him as quite horribly accurate. It gave him, to a degree he had not previously felt, a sense of pariahdom, of being an outcast, a hunted man. It was a peculiarly unpleasant experience.

Raffles gave a slight shrug, and with a shade more of grimness in his expression turned again to the window.

What he saw crushed the radio announcement instantaneously from his mind.

A man in a light grey flannel suit, with a white felt hat in his hand, emerged quickly from the doorway of the Cafe Universal.

The cracksman stood rigid at the window.

Bunny Manders!

Bunny, his partner, was in Gibraltar! Bunny seemed to have been watching Chundra's!

Incredulity was Raffles' first reaction to that brief glimpse of his partner. Then came a fierce, swift exultation. With Bunny here, Bunny on the outside, unsuspected —by heaven, it made a difference!

If he could get in touch with Bunny——

At that moment there was a sharp click, a swishing sound behind him.

Raffles dissimulated the keen sense of relief, of hope, with which the sight of his partner had filled him. Without haste, he turned.

A Hindu, standing with his back to the prayer-rug over the door, faced Raffles across the room. It was that young, slender man in white ducks and narrow black tie whom Raffles had seen holding up the string of amber beads for Drusilla Brook in the back room. Only, seen now at close quarters, it was evident that the man was not so young. The impression of youth came mostly from his slightness of build. His skin, in the duskiness of which there was the faintest tinge of parchment-yellow, was tight over the cheekbones; about his dark, brilliant eyes was a web of fine wrinkles. His wrists were extraordinarily slender, his fingers long, and slim, and dusky, with yellow half-moons in the nails. These details Raffles noticed as the Hindu waved a hand at the window.

"Be so kind, Mr. Raffles," he said, in a light, suave voice, "as to close the shutters."

Raffles did so. Turning back, he saw that the Hindu had not moved. Smiling, showing fine, white teeth, the young-old man said pleasantly:

"I am not, I take it, mistaken in using the name 'Raffles'?"

His English was precise, but almost wholly free of babu characteristics. Raffles said stonily:

"Why should you think that my name is Raffles?"

"My dear sir," the Hindu smiled, "if you prefer the alias of Bell-Evart, by all means let us have it so. But you heard, a minute or two ago, the broadcast of our diligent police chief, Inspector Sacarello. In the circumstances, I should scarcely have thought that Bell-Evart was a name to which you were overly anxious to cling."

Raffles grinned.

"You have me there!"

"I have you every way, Mr. Raffles. I have you, in the English phrase, coming and going. You are a criminal en route to England to stand trial on a charge of robbery with violence. The moment your escape becomes known, you will be wanted, for that, by the English police. You are already wanted by the Gibraltar police for a murder on their territory——"

"Which you committed," Raffles said coolly.

The Hindu spread his slim hands.

"That is a fact. I—or, rather, one of my men acting on my instructions—hurled the stiletto which killed Detective-Inspector Marius. Consider your position, however, as an escaping criminal—and ask yourself what chance you have, if I turn you over to the police with the story that I found you concealed on my premises, of being believed if you accuse me of the murder."

"I have two chances. First, fingerprints on the stiletto hilt——"

"My man will scarcely have been so careless, Mr. Raffles. The other?"

"That the murder was witnessed by a certain lady—a customer who was in your back room"—Raffles was watching the Hindu narrowly—"a Miss Drusilla Brook!"

Lal Chundra's face remained inscrutable.

"The customer you mention—her name means nothing to me—had left the back room some seconds before the death of Marius."

"I see. She had left the room—and the store?"

"And the store, Mr. Raffles."

That, Raffles mentally noted, was a lie. But he did not press the point.

"You grant, then," said Lal Chundra smoothly, "the obvious fact; that I hold you in the hollow of my hand, to turn over to the police—they hang murderers in Gibraltar, Mr. Raffles—or to contrive your escape, whichever I please."

Raffles lighted his cigarette, sat down on a pouffe. He gave the appearance of a man entirely at ease—which, inwardly, he was not!

"You won't be handing me over to the police, Chundra!"

The Hindu sat down on a pouffe opposite him. He leaned a little forward, looking at Raffles with steady, brilliant, dark eyes, his slender hands hanging limp between his knees. The room was shadowy about the two men; the strips of sunlight entering through the shutter did not reach them, but the din of the traffic in Main Street did.

"You are singularly sure of yourself, Mr. Raffles."

"Of course I am. I cannot guess how you know my name; I don't know how you knew Marius' name; I don't know how you knew we were on the *Llandnno Chief*, or that I was Marius' prisoner; I don't know how you knew we should come ashore in Gibraltar today, and I don't know how you knew that we should visit the Bar Monte Cristo. But, Mr. Nanda Lal Chundra," Raffles went on, "all those things quite obviously were familiar to you. And you killed Marius, Chundra, to get me out of his hands; you killed him, and you had me lured here by your crayfish expert, because for some reason you have need of me." Raffles took his cigarette from his lips, smiling. "You say I seem sure of myself. Naturally, I am. You didn't deliver me from the toils of one policeman —Marius—in order to transfer me to the toils of another —Sacarello. Am I right?"

"Perfectly," said the Hindu, "perfectly."

He did not move. His slim hands, with the yellow half-mooned nails, hung lax between his knees as he sat on the pouffe. His dark, large, brilliant eyes, the web of fine wrinkles about them not noticeable in the dimness of the shuttered room, watched Raffles steadily.

"How many persons," he said suddenly, "know your profession, Mr. Raffles—at a rough estimate?"

"I have no profession," said Raffles. "I am a man of independent means—and an amateur of cricket and other sports."

"You include robbery under the heading of 'sports'? Ignoring the relation between your 'independent means' and your considerable gifts as a safebreaker," said the Hindu sweetly, "you would describe yourself, perhaps, as an 'amateur' cracksman? Let us have it so, if you wish. I will put my question differently. How many people, would you say, at a rough estimate, know the relationship between your 'independent means' and your highly profitable hobby of crime?"

"I should have said—six, at the outside. To that number," said Raffles, "I must now add another— yourself."

"I am glad," said Lal Chundra, "that you don't prevaricate. It is important that you and I should understand each other. Yes, I know—and have known for some years—the name of the man behind several of London's neater, more debonair and profitable robberies. Never mind how I knew. I have associations in England. There are several factories there of which I am the virtual owner. And for reasons of my own, the skilful, single-handed cracksman—of whom there are now very few in the world —is of interest to me. Where I hear of him, no matter what his country, I have an eye kept on him. I can sometimes use him, to our mutual profit, on business of my own.

"But for the moment," said Lal Chundra, "leave that. It's sufficient that you should know that, for at least two years, I have been roughly aware of your activities, Mr. Raffles. You are startled?"

"Damnably," Raffles said, with candour. "Go on. This is interesting."

"When you left some months ago for America, using the alias of 'Major Alan Bell-Evart', those of my English associates who were responsible for keeping an eye on you were pardonably intrigued. They arranged for your trail to be picked up on arrival in America. They soon discovered that your object was the almost priceless collection of white jade belonging to the millionaire, Jacob Vanlander."

"Correct," Raffles said cheerfully, "and I still wish I could have got away with it. Vanlander's one of the hardest-boiled pirates unhung; he's ground more necks than your Hindu god, Juggernaut. If I could have got away with that collection, I'd have waited for the reward he'd offer—and I'd have sold his jade back to him for half a million sterling, and done it with a pure heart!"

"However," said Lal Chundra, "the collection proved quite invulnerable—thief-proof. You relinquished the idea. Soon after, you were invited to a house in Westchester County, for the hunting. While there, you heard of the huge sum in cash—a matter of a hundred thousand

—which Mr. Andrew Payne Hulburd, of a neighbouring estate, Forge Park, was reputed always to keep in his safe. To cut a long story short, Mr. Raffles, you cracked that safe. You found the story of the cash to be apocryphal. There was in the safe no cash sum of any importance, but there was something else. You took it, and you got away with it—got away with it so skilfully that it was not until you reached Honolulu that you again appeared within my ken. Just as there are Chundra-controlled factories in Birmingham, England, and the American towns of Buffalo and Seattle—factories engaged in the manufacture of what English call 'small trade-goods' and the Americans call 'notions'—so, in Honolulu, there is a Chundra store. The manager there, as at all Chundra stores, was on the look-out for the globe-trotting 'Major Bell-Evart'.''

Raffles lighted a fresh cigarette.

"The fog," he said gently, "seems to be lifting a little. Chundra, Khitagara & Co. is a 'receiving', a 'fence' organisation on a big scale."

"You might call us so," said Lal Chundra—with an irony in his tone that told Raffles his guess was wrong.

The Hindu continued:

"From Honolulu to Australia, you were again under our eye. You were travelling for two reasons. The first, to confuse your trail and to find a good opportunity to drop your 'Bell-Evart' alias and become again Mr. A. J. Raffles, gentleman. The second, to find a means of disposing profitably of the curious proceeds of your Forge Park robbery. Unfortunately, just at the time when my men were about to establish direct contact with you, an unforeseen event occurred. You were arrested—strangely enough, by an English warrant sworn out in the name of Bell-Evart—in Melbourne."

Raffles grinned.

"Now, we understand each other! You killed Marius at the first opportunity, and you lured me into your hands, because you want the thing that I stole from Forge Park?"

"I want that manuscript," said Lal Chundra, sitting very still. "Marius did not get it from you. I know that. He did not even penetrate your 'Bell-Evart' alias. You have that manuscript, Mr. Raffles. I am not so foolish as to believe that you have it on your person; but you have cached it somewhere on your travels; you know where it is; you know how to re-possess yourself of it. I won't mix my words. Mr. Raffles, I want that manuscript volume which was written by John Drake Weyman, and which you stole from the safe at Forge Park. I may add that I intend to have it."

"So I've noticed," said Raffles. "You've already killed for it." He stood up, paced across the shadowy room, turned. "What's your price?" he said abruptly.

"You are wanted in England on a charge of robbery with violence. You are wanted in Gibraltar for murder. The Rock is mobilised for your capture. Without my help, you have not a chance in the world of escape. Very well, I offer you safety. I will get you out of Gibraltar. I will contrive that every particle of evidence against you, on both charges, is obliterated. I will so arrange matters that you may return to your real identity with no possible chance of subsequent arrest as Bell-Evart. In exchange, you will travel with three of my agents to the country and the place where you have cached the Weyman manuscript. When you place the manuscript in their hands, they will pay to you the sum of ten thousand pounds sterling, in cash. That will conclude our transaction."

Raffles carried his cigarette slowly to his lips, his blue, bold eyes on Nanda Lal Chundra.

The cracksman was more shaken by the offer than he outwardly revealed. His mind went back to that strange night at Forge Park. So that was what had been stolen. A manuscript! A volume written by one John Drake Weyman!

The name meant nothing to Raffles. Yet, because of that theft, of which he was innocent, he had been pursued; he had been arrested; and now, to obtain that manuscript

77

volume on which he, Raffles, had never set eyes, he was offered a chance of escape.

Raffles was a quick thinker. He had perceived swiftly that Chundra's belief that he was the Forge Park robber was a trump card. He had played the card. He had allowed Chundra to continue in his belief that he, Raffles, was the thief. So long as Chundra believed that, he would do what he said—he would contrive Raffles' complete escape from Gibraltar.

To get out of Gibraltar, that was the first and vital thing. Do that, and surely, afterwards, he could handle Chundra's three agents?

These thoughts flickered through Raffles' mind as he gazed at the Hindu.

Lal Chundra's voice broke suddenly through his preoccupation. "Perhaps, Mr. Raffles, this will help you to come to a decision on the terms I have offered you."

Sharply, the Hindu clapped his hands.

With a brief whirring sound, a metallic click, a shutter in the back of a niche in the wall to the left of the door snapped open. The shining barrel of a rifle, with a dark eye sighting along it, covered Raffles through the niche. In the wall to his right, another shutter had opened, another rifle appeared. A third rifle covered him from the wall on his left.

"Silencer-fitted," said Lal Chundra suavely. "With all the traffic out there in Main Street, a rifle report would pass merely as a backfire—very common in this hot climate."

Raffles drew a deep breath.

"I seem to be poorly placed for bargaining," he said. "I accept your terms."

CHAPTER 8

AT THE BURNING GHATS

With that brief sentence, A. J. Raffles signed the death warrant of Inspector Sacarello.

He did not know it. It was impossible for him to know it. He had heard the name Sacarello just once in his life from the loudspeaker.

But when Lal Chundra left the room, after the strange conversation which had culminated in Raffles' acceptance of his terms, the Hindu was already turning over in his mind that guarantee which he had given his prisoner.

"I will contrive," Lal Chundra had said, "that every particle of evidence against you, on both charges, is obliterated."

Lal Chundra was dealing with an acute and skilful man. He had shown that he knew a good deal about Raffles. And he did. Nor was he inclined to underestimate him. Until he, Lal Chundra, had fulfilled his guarantees—had got Raffles out of Gibraltar, obliterated the trail which connected him with "Bell-Evart"—Raffles would not be fool enough to reveal the hiding place of the Weyman Manuscript.

So thought Lal Chundra.

And since he desired the Weyman Manuscript with a cold, merciless, calculating urgency, it was plain to him that the sooner he set about fulfilling his guarantee to Raffles, the quicker he was likely to get his hands on the desired object.

His scheme for getting Raffles out of Gibraltar was already formulated in his mind. Chundra, Khitagara & Co. were experts in the contraband trade with Spain. Impenetrable as this Rock, this small chunk of British territory tacked on to the heel of Spain, might appear, the combined intellects of the British and Spanish authorities had never succeeded in stamping out the contraband traffic. The contrabandists have ways and loopholes of their own; and it was through one of these that Lal Chundra planned to smuggle Raffles.

So much for the first part of his problem.

The second part—that of obliterating evidence—did not present any very much greater difficulty. Lal Chundra had long ago made it his business to be acquainted with Inspector Sacarello. Everybody knows everybody in Gibraltar. Lal Chundra, of the reputable house of Chundra, Khitagara & Co., knew Inspector Sacarello. What was more, he knew all about him—his tastes, his habits, his incorruptibility. He knew—for he had made it his business to find out—infinitely more about Sacarello than Sacarello knew about him. Among other things Chundra knew, was this—that Sacarello was a close friend of Captain Kerry Adam, M.C.; that he habitually made of Captain Adam a confidant.

Sooner or later, Lal Chundra knew, Sacarello would consult Captain Adam in the case of the murdered man, Marius, and the escaped prisoner, Bell-Evart. The consultation would be as between friends, strictly unofficial. It was improbable that Sacarello would ask the captain to come to police headquarters. Therefore, it followed that Sacarello would go to Captain Adam; and since Sacarello respected the captain's knowledge, it followed, further, that he would take with him, for examination by the captain, such evidence, such germane exhibits, as he had so far amassed.

Europa Point, where Captain Adam lived, is one of the few parts of Gibraltar where it is possible to find a comparatively unfrequented road.

Such, then, roughly, were the thoughts, the plans, of Nanda Lal Chundra immediately following his interview with Raffles.

The cracksman's thoughts were far otherwise. He did now know that, by his acceptance of Lal Chundra's terms, he had to all intents signed Sacarello's death warrant. He did not think about Sacarello at all. The name did not enter his head.

Left alone in the room over the Hindu store, his first thought was of the brief glimpse he had had of his partner Bunny Manders.

The moment the prayer-rug had swung back into place over the door through which the Hindu had just passed, Raffles crossed quickly to the window, unlatched the shutters, drew one of them a trifle open.

The traffic in the narrow canyon of the street was appreciably less; the pavements were not so crowded. Those hundreds of white-clad tourists who had invaded Gibraltar that morning were now returned to their ship.

Raffles reflected, grimly, that with one of its passengers dead, and another hunted as the murderer, the *Llandnno Chief* would probably be delayed. For himself, it would suit Raffles fine if he never saw the *Llandnno Chief* again; he'd had enough of that ship to last him a lifetime.

He stood watching, through the crack between the shutters, the doorway of the Cafe Universal, opposite. The band was still playing there; sob of saxes, squeal of fiddles, rattle of castanets. Groups of sailors, soldiers and marines passed in and out. Four husky Naval police, in white uniforms and short gaiters, came and planted themselves with gloomy majesty outside the cafe door.

There was no sign of Bunny.

Raffles could guess why his partner had come to Gib. He had hoped to be able to do something—to engineer Raffles' escape. Bunny must have seen him enter Chundra's, and he had kept watch on the place. Now, Raffles thought, he must have given it up; probably Bunny thought he had left by some back way. Anyway, there was no sign of Bunny, now.

In any case, Raffles reflected, there was nothing Bunny could have done to help. Raffles' one real chance was Chundra. Chundra thought he knew the whereabouts of the Weyman Manuscript. So thinking, Chundra would keep his bargain; with his knowledge of the place, its underground ways and secret loopholes, Chundra would get him out of Gib if anybody could.

His own side of the bargain Raffles could not possibly

keep. He had never set eyes on the Weyman Manuscript. Chundra was going to turn dangerous when he found out the truth. Let him. Raffles would cross that bridge when he came to it. He had never before in his life made a bargain that he could not keep. But when a man's life and freedom is at stake, and the other party to a bargain is a cunning killer quite prepared to pin his own crime on you, you're not apt to be over particular.

Raffles closed the shutters, turned from the window, stretched himself at full length on a divan, lighted a cigarette. He suspected that all the time, through some peephole in one or other of the wall-niches, he was under observation. That didn't worry him. He had a cold-drawn nerve. He showed it presently by rearranging the cushions to his liking, and, deliberately making his mind a blank, dropping off to sleep.

While Raffles slept, Inspector Sacarello received the cable which revealed the fact that the dead man, Marius, was not and had never been a Yard operative, and that the Bell-Evart warrant was fake.

While Raffles slept, Bunny Manders and Dan Westray joined forces, and, seeking Drusilla Brook, went to the docks—and were detained by Sergeant Mifsud.

While Raffles slept, Inspector Sacarello went to his death, and Blake, of Baker Street—"resting" after three weeks of hard, dangerous work in Tangier—found a new case on his hands.

Of all these things, A. J. Raffles, sleeping, remained ignorant.

When he awoke, it was the touch of a hand on his shoulder. He sat up quickly. Light from the Moorish chandelier filled the room. Lal Chundra, spreading out a number of articles on a small table nearby, smiled with a flash of white teeth.

"I salute your nerve. Not many men, placed as you are, could sleep so peacefully."

"It's the Bonaparte touch," said Raffles.

He became aware that the sound of traffic in Main Street was now missing. He glanced at his watch.

"Half-past eleven!"

"Much has been done," said the Hindu. "You will be glad to hear that the little matter of the obliteration of evidence has already been taken care of. It was as well. I found that my knife-throwing employee had actually been so careless as to leave a fingerprint on the stiletto hilt. That may cause me some slight complication later. It will not affect you, however."

"What the devil have you been up to?"

"It was no part of our bargain, Mr. Raffles, that I should notify you of such steps as I deem it advisable to take." He indicated the things he had placed on the table. "I want you, first, to shave your moustache. Then —you are familiar with the use of make-up?"

"I've had some experience with it," Raffles grinned.

"Good. All the materials are here. Here, too, is a change of clothes. With the addition of these tinted glasses—your eyes being, unfortunately, blue—you should, I think, make a passable addition to my race, Mr.—shall we say?—Mr. Rabaji Ram Dass!"

"Oah, decidedlee," he said.

"Your clothes, you will notice," said the Hindu, "are of the hue of mourning. There is purpose in this. Gibraltar has a considerable Hindu population. Our place of cremation, our burning-ghats, has been long set aside for us. It is on the other side of the Rock, in the neighbourhood of a curious, tiny colony of fishermen's houses, called Catalan Bay. Except for that handful of cottages, huddling together, and the Hindu burning-ghats, there is nothing at all on the other side of the Rock; it is given over entirely to water catchments."

Raffles was busy with brush and lather at a small shaving mirror on the low table. "What's the plan?"

"Hindu mourners frequently visit the burning-ghats at midnight. It is a custom."

"And Mr. Rabaji Ram Dass I take it, has suffered a recent bereavement?"

"Precisely. The burning-ghats," continued the Hindu, "back upon the sea. A fishing boat from Catalan Bay will be waiting to take you off. Three of my men will go with you. It is a small boat; your passage will not be luxurious."

"Will it be a long one?"

"Two hundred and thirty miles. You are going to Oran, in Algeria!"

Down Main Street, a little later, there clip-clopped a white-canopied horse-carriage. On the headstall of the horse, there nodded sombrely three black ostrich plumes. The wheels were rubber-shod, silent; the horse's hoofs echoed hollowly in the narrow, deserted street, sloping steeply down between the tall buildings with their small balconies and shuttered windows.

The street lamps were few and pale; but the moon, sailing high over the roofs, checkered the street with silver light and sable shadow.

The canvas side curtains of the high, top-heavy carriage were rolled up, showing that it was empty. A policeman, his blue, London uniform and helmet somehow incongruous in these surroundings, noted the black plumes on the horse's head, saw the carriage draw up outside the Hindu store of Chundra, Khitagara & Co., and, being a Gibraltarian, guessed that the carriage was going to the burning-ghats. He stood watching.

In the big roll shutter which was drawn down over the window of the store, a small wicket door opened. Four Hindus, in black suits, white shirts and narrow black ties—one of them wearing tinted glasses—emerged into the moonlight. The last closed the wicket carefully. The four men climbed into the carriage, which clip-clopped away down towards the Water Gate.

P.C. Carreras resumed his round with no idea that he had just conspiciously failed to arrest the urgently-wanted Major Alan Bell-Evart!

The carriage, meantime, passed under the Water Gate, rolled through the small square hemmed in by the grey walls of the old-time batteries, and came out on to a road running between public gardens filled with palm trees and ornamental shrubs.

This was the road to the British Gate, through which

you pass on to No Man's Land and thence into Spain. But the carriage turned to the right, into a road running along at the foot of a sheer, naked, towering precipice of gigantic proportions—the end of the Rock. With that incongruity which makes Gibraltar unique, here, huddled at the foot of the precipice, were a leper colony, a cricket ground, a racecourse, and, further on, the Hindu burning-ghats.

The carriage sped on silent wheels along the flat road, the clip-clop of the horse's hoofs clear and echoing. The three Hindus and the man who looked like a Hindu sat two to a seat, facing each other. None spoke. They had not rolled down the side curtains, and the glim of the guttering candle lamps each side of the driver's box occasionally fell across the face first of one man, then of another.

Rabaji Ram Dass pushed up his tinted, horn-rimmed spectacles on to his dusky forehead, and his eyes—the blue, bold eyes of A. J. Raffles—studied, at such times as the gleam from the lamps gave him the opportunity, the faces of his captors.

These agents of Lal Chundra—who had himself remained behind—were, Raffles judged, pretty competent cut-throats. They were, of course, armed—which Raffles was not—and they looked like men who would know how to use their weapons. Their job was to get him aboard the fishing-smack, guard him every moment of the voyage to Oran, and deliver him up to Chundra's agents in that Algerian town.

This was the strangest situation in which the cracksman had ever found himself.

He peered out from the carriage. The mighty precipice, which dwarfed the carriage to the proportions of a toy, cut off the moonlight. To the right of the carriage the feeble glim of the candle lamp shone occasionally on a wall of naked rock. To the left was a low, railed fence—that of the racecourse, for once the light shone dimly on a notice: "GIBRALTAR JOCKEY CLUB, MEMBERS' ENCLOSURE." Though nothing was to be seen of them, three thousand refugees from the civil war were encamped on that racecourse, Gibraltar's one great open space.

Not far beyond the racecourse, the carriage at last drew up. The man beside Raffles climbed down. The two on the opposite seat remained there facing him.

"Descend," one of them said.

The gleam from the candle lamps showed Raffles that the two men facing him, and the one who waited for him beside the carriage, each held a pistol thrust forward in the pocket of his black jacket.

They were taking no chances.

Raffles descended, joining the man in the road. Instantly the two others followed. One of them spoke quickly to the driver, who turned his horse, cracked his whip. On silent wheels the carriage sped away over the road by which it had come.

The four men stood there for a moment in a little group. They were at a point where the road curved round the side of the Rock, following the foot of the precipice. To the left of the road was the sea—the Mediterranean. Main Street, and the town itself, from which they had come, lay right over on the other side of the Rock—the Atlantic side.

A hand closed on Raffles' arm, above the elbow.

"Come!"

It was totally black here, under the looming precipice, though far out the sea heaved vaguely silver. Raffles' feet sank in yielding, parched sand, which, as his eyes grew accustomed to the blackness, he dimly made out to be tussocked with clumps of dune grass.

Though so near to the sea, no breath of air stirred; a humid heat, equal almost to that of a Turkish bath, brought out the moisture in the palms of his hands and on his forehead. He hoped Lal Chundra's make-up was of good quality.

They must, he calculated, have walked fifty yards from the road when a high, white wall glimmered up ahead out of the blackness. Drawing closer, he made out a pair of high, wrought-iron gates under an Oriental arch.

One of the Hindus plucked a bell-pull to the left of the gates. Forlornly the tolling of the bell sounded through the dark, stifling silence.

Some minutes passed, then the gleam of a candle lantern fell across the bars of the gate, and a stooped, hooded figure slowly approached. From under her white hood the wrinkled, dark face of a toothless, aged Hindu woman peered through the bars at them, the caste-mark visible on her brow as she held up her candle lantern.

One of the Hindus spoke to her swiftly in her own tongue, and, nodding, she opened the gates a crack. They passed through in single file, one man ahead of Raffles, two behind him.

The old woman refastened the gates carefully, stooped at the lock, the candle lantern burning tremorless on the sand at her feet.

Ignoring her, the three men, hemming Raffles in, pressed forward over the dunes.

Again they were in darkness. Here and there loomed, vaguely, black piles of stones—burnt-out funeral pyres. Everywhere was a smell of ashes. Once their approach disturbed some great bird, which hopped clumsily ahead of them, and with a strange, evil croak, spread wide wings and soared into the night. A vulture, Raffles realised; and a moment later, stopping his heart, there broke out, somewhere ahead, a wailing, sorrowful cry, eerie, mournful and piteous.

As they topped the swell of a dune, ahead and away to their left they saw the red, flickering glow of a fire, visible through the interstices of a low, round tower of stones in which it burned—and against the glow a ring of shawled, bowed figures showed black: mourners, chanting on the weird semi-tone scale of the East.

The four men did not approach the fire, but bore away to the left.

Presently they came to another wall, which one man swiftly scaled. He vanished on the other side. With the two others, Raffles waited. Through the sound of the mournful, eerie chanting, he could hear the cool, clean, quiet murmur of small waves breaking nearby along a sandy shore.

The sullen glow of that funeral-pyre, the chanting, the smell of ashes and of smoke——

He hungered to get out of this place, out on to the clean, cool sea.

From the far side of the wall came a sibilant hissing sound. One of the Hindus touched Raffles' arm.

"Climb!"

He scaled the wall easily, dropped lightly into the sand on the far side. The Hindu who had gone ahead was waiting for him. The other two dropped down quickly beside them.

They were on a narrow strip of beach, under the wall of the burning ghats. One of the Hindus leading the way, they walked along quickly in single file under the wall, then cut across the beach. The figure of a man loomed up, standing by a dinghy drawn in with its bows beached on the sand.

One of the Hindus leaped quickly into the boat. Another touched Raffles' arm. "Enter!"

He made to obey. He had one foot in the boat when a warning hiss from one of the Hindus checked him. Still as statues in the darkness, the five men listened.

Footsteps sounded, brushing through the sand, approaching. Suddenly they stopped.

Raffles held his breath. He did not move a muscle. Not one of the five men moved. He could see nothing.

Suddenly, peremptorily, a voice rang out, in pure Cockney:

"'Altoogozeair?"

Silence. Only the rustle of the small waves along the beach. The thud of Raffles' heart checked off the seconds.

Clear, peremptory, the voice came again:

"I sees yer! Speak up, or I shoot!"

One of the Hindus made a swift movement, a knife gleamed for an instant flat on the palm of his hand as he crouched, peering into the blackness. His hand went back to hurl the knife, and Raffles' fist smashed into the man's face, felling him like an ox, his head and shoulders coming down with a splash in the water.

That action of Raffles' was instinctive. He was a Britisher, so was the Tommy.

Raffles knocked the Hindu cold, and flung himself flat on the sand, knowing what was coming.

It came—a volley of good Poplar swearwords, a blue-white flash from a rifle, an echoing report.

Behind Raffles, the boatman coughed once, reeled, folded up over the gunwale of his boat, his feet trailing in the water.

High up on the Rock the white blaze of a searchlight leaped out, answering that rifle-shot. The glare leaped downward, raced along the seashore, and in an instant picked out the boat, the Hindu standing in it, the figure dangling over its gunwale, the two other Hindus and Raffles flat on the sand, the sentry, in khaki shorts and pith helmet, on one knee under the wall, rifle levelled, and a second sentry tearing along the beach.

And as the searchlight illumined the scene, one of the Hindus snapped out an automatic, fired, and the sentry under the wall pitched forward on his face.

The three Hindus and Raffles leaped simultaneously to their feet and ran, the other sentry coming up from the other way along the beach.

He stopped, levelled his rifle, fired.

The Hindu running beside Raffles stumbled forward, fell—hit squarely between the shoulders.

Next second Raffles found himself out of the glare, running for his life in pitch blackness. He veered to the right, came up against the wall of the burning ghats, scaled it, dropped down on the inside.

For a moment he crouched there, trying to still his heavy breathing, trying to listen.

The chanting had ceased. Dead silence. No sign of the Hindus. Then, far along the beach to his right, a rifle report rang out.

Raffles broke into a crouching run, following the wall of the burning-ghats, on the inside, in pitch blackness.

CHAPTER 9

ALL CLUES VANISH

At the head of Main Street, where that steep, narrow, semi-Oriental thoroughfare widens out into a small square, stands Government House. No grounds separate it from the street. Its two-storied brick facade rises direct from the pavement. It is neither an impressive nor a striking building, but a diminutive round tower, with crenelations, which juts out from the facade at the level of the second-storey windows lends to it a certain appearance of official significance. A sentry-box to either side of the entrance heightens this official look.

Facing it across the street is the naval picket house, a low, grey building with two acacia trees in front of it, a flagstaff, and a pair of obsolete field-guns with white-washed wheels and highly polished brasswork. The white-uniformed, short-gaitered, bandoliered, rifle-bearing naval sentry here faces the two pith-helmeted sentries in front of Government House opposite.

As a display of imperial might, the scene is inadequate. Tourists, who have been familiar all their lives with the phrase "Safe as the Rock of Gibraltar", are apt to be disappointed in it; just as they are surprised to find that Gibraltar itself is far more like a town in Spanish Morocco than a British fortress.

Yet Government House is far more important than it looks. It is, first, the nerve-centre of British activity in the Western Mediterranean: in itself, a tall order. Second, though Gibraltar with its large civil population possesses its own legislature, its own system of jurisprudence, its own supreme court, the veto of Government House overrules all.

The governor has the last word. His influence is all-powerful.

A good hour before Raffles left Chundra, Khitagara &

Co.'s for the burning-ghats—while, in fact, he still slept in that room over the Hindu store—a black Hillman Minx hummed to a standstill in the moonlight outside Government House.

It was the car familiar to all Gibraltar as Inspector Sacarello's. But the little detective was not in it. A keen-faced, grey-eyed youngster was at the wheel; beside him sat a tall, aquiline, sunburned man with dark hair deeply receded over the temples, and a pipe clamped between his teeth. In the back was an Army officer, heavily built, pink-faced, with a yellow toothbrush moustache.

The two sentries sprang smartly to the salute, the moonlight gleaming on their naked bayonets, as the Army officer and the tall civilian descended from the car.

The tall man said to the youngster at the wheel:

"Shan't be long, Tinker."

The bulky officer—Captain Kerry Adam—acknowledged the sentries' salutes, pressed a bell-push, and through a wicket which opened in the big doors the two men entered Government House.

Tinker settled himself comfortably to wait.

It was half an hour before Blake and Captain Adam emerged from Government House. The result of the highly important interview which had just occurred was not apparent in Blake's face, which was quite inscrutable as he took his seat in the car. But when he said briefly, "Police station", Tinker knew with a thrill that the interview had been satisfactory.

"Straight on," said Captain Adam. "First to the left, first to the right. It's next to the public baths." He leaned back on the rear seat as the car hummed forward, and added: "Well, that's that, Blake."

The criminologist loaded his pipe thoughtfully, set it between his teeth.

"That," he agreed, "is that. Nobody more loathes publicity than I do, but there are times when it's useful to have a reputation."

"You're in charge, guv'nor?" Tinker asked quickly.

"Not officially," Blake said. "A certain Inspector

Parodi will be acting police chief in Inspector Sacarello's place; therefore, he'll be officially in charge of the investigation into his late chief's death. But actually a certain influence will be brought to bear, and complete official collaboration will be given to me. In effect, I shall have a free hand. It's a rather delicate situation. I hope Inspector Parodi is not going to resent it."

But, partly because the Government House telephone wire had been busy, and even more because Inspector Parodi, too, knew Blake by reputation, there was no hint of resentment in the greeting the criminologist received at police headquarters.

On the contrary, Inspector Parodi was unfeignedly glad to have Blake on the job, and said so.

"I have my hands full with the refugee problem—three thousand of them camped down there on the racecourse alone," he said. "Gibraltar's a city of strange faces just now, Mr. Blake."

"Yes," Blake said thoughtfully; "a city of strange faces." That was a fact, he judged, which was not going to make his job any easier—all those strange faces. "By the way," he said, "just how much have the newspapermen got?"

"I don't know, Mr. Blake. There have been a lot of them here—English newspapermen. Inspector Sacarello spoke to them, but just what he told them I don't know. This Bell-Evart business has developed very rapidly. Por Dios"—as with all Gibraltarians, Spanish came unbidden to Parodi's tongue, and his English had a faint accent— "the *Llandnno Chief* only arrived late this morning!"

"And nobody knows," Blake said, "just how much Inspector Sacarello had learned. He'd not had time to make any report to Government House."

Loading his pipe, he sat on the edge of Inspector Sacarello's desk, swinging one long, white-flannelled leg, his grey deep-set eyes looking round the room.

All that Blake knew, to date, was what he had learned from the police surgeon, Dr. Azzopardi, who had come out to Captain Adam's bungalow, in answer to the captain's 'phone-call, to take charge of Inspector Sacarello's body.

Blake had seized the opportunity to inquire of Dr. Azzopardi if he knew what was behind the radio announcement concerning Major Bell-Evart. The doctor had told him, then, of the death of the man Marius from the *Llandnno Chief*, and the disappearance of his companion, Bell-Evart. Further, Dr. Azzopardi had told Blake what he had heard of Inspector Sacarello's questioning of the proprietor of the Monte Cristo Bar, Garcia, and the waiter, Jose; and told him, also, of Sacarello's discovery that the dead man, Marius, was a Scotland Yard detective, and that Bell-Evart was his prisoner.

That, and the fact that Marius had been killed by a stiletto with an ivory, elephant-head hilt, on which there had been one single fingerprint, was all Blake knew when, at the urgent request of Sacarello's friend, Captain Adam, he offered his services at Government House. And it was all that he knew now, as his eyes turned from their scrutiny of the dead inspector's office to meet the anxious regard of Inspector Parodi.

Parodi was a young man, under thirty, slender of stature, dark-skinned, rather goodlooking, but—as the drawn lines in his face betrayed—badly overworked. Blake noted the fact. He said:

"Don't take a word of advice amiss, inspector, but if the Sacarello business is all that's holding you here, I'd get home and snatch some sleep, if I were you."

"I can do with it," Parodi admitted. "May I suggest that you use Inspector Sacarello's office here? And if you need any assistance, my men are instructed to put themselves at your disposal."

The moment Parodi was gone, Blake seated himself in the desk chair, began to try the drawers of the desk. All were unlocked, except one.

In a corner of the room was a massive, but rather old-fashioned safe. This, too, when Tinker tried it on Blake's instructions, proved to be locked.

"Go and ask the sergeant in the charge-room for Sacarello's keys," Blake told Tinker. "He's got everything that was found in Sacarello's pockets."

"What are you after?" asked Captain Adam.

"A working hypothesis," Blake said. "What do we know? First, that Detective-Inspector Marius, C.I.D., comes ashore with a prisoner, Major Alan Bell-Evart, whom he's taking home for trial. Second, Marius is killed, Bell-Evart disappears. Third, Inspector Sacarello gathers together certain exhibits relating to the case—the stiletto with which the murder was committed; the contents of the dead man's pockets; the dead man's warrant-card, and his warrant for Bell-Evart. Fourth, Inspector Sacarello is murdered. He's murdered at your gate. Why was he coming to see you? Because he's in the habit of consulting you in important cases. Would it be likely that he brought with him such exhibits, or clues, as he had so far gathered? Certainly it would be likely, since—as we suppose—he had come to lay the facts before you and to ask your opinion.

"Hence," Blake said, puffing at his pipe, "if the exhibits are not here, then the probability that he took them with him to your bungalow becomes a certainty. But they were not found on his body or in his car. Therefore, if they are not here, they were taken from him by the murderer; and it's probable that to obtain them was the murderer's motive in striking him down.

"It follows," Blake went on, "that if we are correct so far, then there was among the exhibits a definite clue which the murderer desired to destroy. A clue to what? A clue to the mystery of the first murder, that of Marius. Therefore, the murder of Marius and the murder of Sacarello are interlinked. Which is tantamount to saying that they were committed by the same man.

"Who killed Marius? Every probability points to the fact that his prisoner, Bell-Evart, killed him. Why? To escape—to evade trial in England on whatever charge it is that originally brought about his arrest by Marius. But if Bell-Evart killed Marius, then—since we've reasoned it out that the same man killed Sacarello—Bell-Evart is guilty of the second crime, also. We've seen that, on probability, his motive for the second murder was the destruction of a piece of evidence relating to the first murder. And that's where the chain of reasoning becomes complicated, and one can dignify the case with the word 'mystery'."

"Why?" said the Army detective.

"For this reason," Blake said. "If Bell-Evart killed Marius, circumstantial evidence alone—the mere fact that Marius was taking Bell-Evart home to prison, and Bell-Evart's consequent escape motive—is enough to hang the man. He must know it. Wherever he may have concealed himself in this town, he must have heard those radio announcements. He must know they're after him. Therefore, what possible piece of evidence can have fallen into Sacarello's hands to prompt Bell-Evart to commit a second murder? It doesn't make sense.

"Again, how did Bell-Evart—if it was Bell-Evart who killed Sacarello—how did he know that Sacarello would visit you and take the evidence with him? I grant you that a Gibraltarian, a native of the place, might be familiar with Sacarello's habits—know of his friendship with you and of his custom of consulting you. But Bell-Evart? I don't see it, captain. The man only came ashore here this morning. Unless he was familiar—very familiar—with Gibraltar and its people before his arrival here today, I don't see how Bell-Evart can have known of Sacarello's friendship with you."

"Bell-Evart uses the title 'Major'," the army detective pointed out. "He may at some time have been stationed on the Rock."

"Have you looked him up in the 'Army List'?" Blake asked.
"No."

"I have," said Blake—"in your own 'Army List', while you were 'phoning Government House to make our appointment there. 'Bell-Evart' may or not be an alias; as 'Major', certainly, he's self-styled. He's not in the 'Army List'—and I incline to the opinion that the entire name, 'Major Alan Bell-Evart', is self-assumed."

Tinker, who had returned with Inspector Sacarello's keys, and had stood listening, broke in eagerly:

"I know why, guv'nor! It's because of the way that radio description of Bell-Evart fits——"

"Fits," Blake said gently, "that astute cracksman with whom we've once before crossed swords—A. J. Raffles!"

Captain Adam sat up.

"Raffles the cricketer!"

"The same," Blake said. "Raffles the cricketer, my dear Adam, is the most elusive crook in England. The Yard knows it, and I know it—but neither they nor I have been able to bring him to trial. I've met him just once. You might call the result a draw. I've looked forward very keenly, ever since, to crossing his trail again. I like him; I can't help a certain admiration for him, but I intend to put him behind bars one of these days—and he knows it!

"However," Blake went on, "we've only this resemblance between their descriptions to lead us to believe that Bell-Evart may be Raffles. We'll wait till we've something more definite to go on before we jump to conclusions. Now, then—let's have those keys, Tinker."

Captain Adam watched sombrely while the criminologist and his assistant went through the desk drawers and the safe of his late friend, Inspector Horacio Sacarello. The captain had had a genuine affection for the little inspector. He still felt the tingling horror of that moment when, following the loud, clear knock on the garden door, the small man had fallen stone-dead into his arms. According to Dr. Azzopardi, actual death had been due to heart-failure, following semi-strangulation. The assailant had probably left the little man for dead, whereas he was not dead, but in a coma. There was no saying how long this condition may have lasted, but somehow the little man had contrived after a time to regain his feet, to knock once on the door. His heart, in Dr. Azzopardi's view, must have failed him practically in the moment that he knocked.

It was a sombre reflection for Captain Adam that, while he had been bullyragging his batman, about the radio and the leg of lamb, his friend had been gasping out his life twenty yards away.

96

The soldier's eyes were hard as he watched Blake's expert, thorough examination of Sacarello's effects. It did not take long. When it was finished, Blake swung shut the heavy door of the safe, returned to his desk chair.

"Well, that's that," he said. "The stiletto is not here; Marius' warrant-card and his warrant for Bell-Evart, and all other exhibits Sacarello may have collected, are conspicuous by their absence. In other words—all clues have vanished! So that our working hypothesis—namely, that the two murders are interlinked, and Bell-Evart killed Sacarello to destroy some vital piece of evidence relating to the murder of Marius—must stand. That's what we've got to go to work on. To investigate the murder of Sacarello, we've got first to investigate the murder of Marius. And for an excellent start, all clues to the murder of Marius have vanished—except one: the photograph of the fingerprint on the stiletto hilt. The fingerprint's not in the records here; that's been ascertained. It'll have to be sent to the Yard; a reply will take four or five days; and I'm not very hopeful of it. Beyond that, all that's left are Marius' and Bell-Evart's suitcases, which Sacarello took charge of from the ship—and Inspector Parodi says that they're entirely barren of information."

"What do you plan to do?" Captain Adam asked.

"The entire Rock," Blake said, "is mobilised to locate and seize Bell-Evart. There's nothing more I can do in that direction. All that's left for me is to go again over the ground Sacarello's already been over. I must go to the ship, question the captain, and so on, and I must examine the death room in the Bar Monte Cristo, and the proprietor and waiter. After that—we shall see!"

He rose. Captain Adam twitched back his khaki cuff to look at his watch.

"It's ten minutes after midnight," he said.

Blake grinned.

"I regret my bed, but that can't be helped. I'm afraid I shall have to make the captain of the *Llandnno Chief* and the proprietor and waiter of the Bar Monte Cristo regret theirs, too! We dare not lose time. Right now, Bell-Evart may be slipping out of Gib under our noses!"

"Not a chance," Captain Adam said positively. "Why he hasn't been brought in already passes my comprehension; but one thing I'm sure of—with the civilian police, the dock police, the naval and military sentries, a blinkin' mouse couldn't get off this Rock unseen! Man, this is Gibraltar—and with special precautions in every corner, at that, on account of the Spanish fighting next door! Bell-Evart hasn't a cat's chance!"

Blake said nothing to that.

Captain Adam parted from them outside the police station. Military duties took him to his office in Bombhouse Lane, nearby, to receive reports. On the Rock, this formidable mountain-top thrust up out of the southern sea, this precipice bristling with armaments that kept open the straits, the trade routes to the East, the vital arteries of England, there were eyes that never slept.

As though to point this fact, as Captain Adam's echoing footsteps died away down the quiet by-street, and Blake stood on the pavement filling his pipe before entering the Hillman, high up on the Rock, which towered above the huddled roofs, the scattered groups of palm trees, and the street where he stood, there shone out suddenly a white glow that dimmed the moonlight.

For a second he was puzzled—then realised that it was the reflection of a searchlight playing silently away over on the other side of the Rock.

He watched the glow, for a space, with interest—but, not being possessed of second sight, did not connect it with the case that engaged his attention. Neither did he attach any personal significance to the motor-ambulance which, a few minutes later, as the Hillman was about to enter Main Street, roared with clanging bell down that steep, narrow, deserted thoroughfare.

Both Blake and his assistant saw the ambulance flash by.

"Army," Tinker said. "Wonder what's happened? Lord, guv'nor, there's something about this place that makes me tingle all over!"

"And we came here," Blake said dryly, "for a 'rest'!"

The wild echoes of the ambulance bell seemed to vibrate in the silence of Main Street as the Hillman purred down it and, following Captain Adam's directions, turned into the alley where stood the Bar Monte Cristo.

As the car's headlights blazed white through the blackness of the alley, for a fraction of a second a figure crouched on the top of a whitewashed wall far along was visible in sharp silhouette. Next instant, as Tinker jammed on the Hillman's brakes, the figure vanished dropping down on the inside of the wall.

Tinker switched off the engine, but left the headlights on. They blazed down the narrow, sloping alley in a silence strangely menacing. Tinker spoke tensely:

"See that?"

"I saw it," Blake said. His keen eyes marked the spot on the wall where he had seen the prowler. "Switch off— and wait here!"

As the lights snapped out Blake stepped from the car and walked quickly down the alley.

It was pitch black. The roofs of the tall, whitewashed buildings each side almost met. Looking up, he saw between them a ribbon of sky, sewn with stars, but neither starshine nor moonlight entered this alley.

In the instant before Tinker had snapped off the headlights Blake had taken note of the building to either side. The one on his left, as a hanging sign had shown, was the Bar Monte Cristo; that on the right, facing it, bore painted on its white wall, which was blank but for one shuttered window at ground level, the legend:

CHUNDRA, KHITAGARA & CO.,
INDIA STORES.

The alley was dead silent.

As far as Blake had been able to make out in his snap appraisal of the scene, the building on his right—Chundra's—presented a five-storey front to Main Street; behind that it stretched some way back along the alley at the height only of two storeys; behind that again was what probably would prove to be a walled garden or yard.

It was on the wall at this point that the prowler had been crouched.

As he neared the spot Blake moved with increased caution, listening intently. His right hand, thrust into his blue double-breasted coat, loosened the big automatic in the holster which fitted snugly under his left armpit. He slipped the safety-catch, peering up at the top of the wall which, whitewashed, glimmered ghostly in the blackness.

No sound came from beyond the wall.

It was not high at this point. Blake, a tall man, by reaching up could grasp the top of it.

He did not hesitate. The prowler he had seen might be merely some sneak-thief; he might be nothing more than one of those homeless refugees of whom Gibraltar was just now filled—some poor devil seeking a doss in someone's backyard. On the other hand, the Bar Monte Cristo, containing the room, now sealed up by the police—in which Detective-Inspector Marius had died, was nearby. Prowlers in the vicinity of the Bar Monte Cristo would bear investigation.

Blake's lean, strong fingers gripped the top of the wall. Soundlessly he drew himself up, threw a leg over the wall, and next moment was seated on top of it, peering down into blackness. That blackness was impenetrable. The windows at the back of the building showed no chink of light. Not a sound broke the hot stillness, which was strongly scented with Eau de Cologne.

That reek of perfume gave Blake a vivid imaginative image of what was before him here in the darkness. Not a garden. A walled yard—the backyard of the Hindu store, where incoming goods were unpacked. A bottle of Eau de Cologne had been recently broken there. He pictured the yard littered with straw and shattered packing-cases, and, lowering himself from the wall, exercised extreme care as to where he put his feet.

He landed in the yard quite soundlessly; but, as he took a step forward from the wall, sure enough his foot struck with a startling clatter against a piece of wood. Like a shaft of lightning a flashlamp blazed whitely into his eyes, blinding him. In an instant, dazzled as he was, he had whipped his automatic from its armpit-holster; but, before he could use his weapon, a clenched fist smashed down from the left on the wrist of his gun-hand, jerking the automatic from his fingers.

There were two men here!

Blake ducked, aimed a terrific kick at the flashlamp, and connected. But as, with a gasp of pain from the man who had held it, the light arced into the air and fell and smashed, a shattering blow on the side of the head knocked Blake sprawling. He clutched at a shadowy figure, felt a sudden, burning pain in his right hand, tripped—and went down, half-stunned.

Ten seconds later Tinker, standing stockstill in the black alley some yards from the car, heard two thuds, as of men dropping lightly from a wall, followed instantly by a rush of running footsteps, receding down the alley.

Tinker turned, darted back to the Hillman, reached in, snapped on the headlights. The glare cut a swathe through the blackness down the sloping alley—showed up a shuttered building, marked "PANERIA", in the cross-street cutting across the alley mouth.

But the alley was empty.

Next second Blake appeared on the wall. Tinker left the Hillman's headlights on, ran forward in the glare, reached Blake as the tall detective dropped down into the alley.

"They went that way, guv'nor—two of 'em!"

Blake glanced down the alley. He shrugged, and, brushing the white dust from his blue double-breasted coat, said quietly!"

"Well, they've got away with it, son—this time!"

"I didn't get a look at 'em," Tinker said. "Did——"
He broke off. "What's the matter with your right hand, guv'nor?"

Blake was using his left hand to brush off his coat. He kept his right hand clenched shut, but between the brown, lean fingers there was trickling, clearly visible in the shine of the headlights, thin ribbons of blood.

Blake went on brushing off his coat. In the studiedly quiet tone which, Tinker knew, was always a sign in his chief of intense excitement, he said:

"From the moment we first heard Inspector Sacarello's radio description of Major Alan Bell-Evart, we were struck by its resemblance to that of A. J. Raffles. Am I right?"

"Sure!"

"D'you remember his partner, Manders—Bunny Manders?"

"You bet!"

"What d'you remember chiefly about him?"

"I dunno," said Tinker—"except that he's a bit of a dude, with eyeglass, an' all that, but not such a fool as he looks."

"'Eyeglass' is the salient word," said Blake. "Bell-Evart's resemblance to Raffles might have been a coincidence. But to ascribe this to coincidence would be to stretch it a little too far!"

He opened his right hand suddenly. On the lacerated palm lay the blood-stained fragments of a monocle.

CHAPTER 10

KNIVES ARE TRUMPS

THAT cross-street which cut across the alley at its lower end runs parallel with Main Street, and is called, somewhat quaintly, "Irish Town". Like all Gibraltar's streets, except those out at the newer end, toward Europa Point, it is extremely narrow—even narrower than most. Hemmed in between high, flat-fronted, shabby buildings, sunlight touched it only for a brief space at noon. Its buildings are the establishments of "general merchants". Airless, it is never free of the strong odours of tobacco, garlic, carbon monoxide and decaying fruit; and, for all its name, you could hunt for a week and find never an Irishman.

Along this street, thankful for its indifferent lighting, sped the two prowlers whom Blake had interrupted in the backyard of Messrs. Chundra, Khitagara & Co. They ran practically without sound, one in shoes with soles of crepe rubber, the other in light dress pumps—and frequently they glanced back.

The runners darted soon into another alley, turning to the right off the street called Irish Town. This second alley was pitch-black. The runners entered it in a manner only to be described as precipitate. Quite different was the manner of their emergence at the other end.

Here the alley opened into what was, for Gibraltar, quite a wide road, with houses only on one side. The opposite side was open to the broad though grassless expanse of the Naval Cricket Ground, and beyond that to the harbour, the curving sea wall, and all the vast expanse of Algeciras Bay.

The two men who so precipitately had entered the other end of the alley emerged at this end with all the appearance of leisured saunterers. One, built on slighter lines than his companion, and with blond, smooth hair, wore a faultless double-breasted dinner-jacket, with turn-down collar. The other long, loose-limbed, yellow-haired, wore white ducks.

They crossed the road to the opposite side, where a broad, paved walk, lined with palm trees and street lamps, looked down over the cricket ground. A cool breeze came in off the wide bay; the water shone silver under the moonlight. Far out, far off across the bay, the mountains of Spain were just visible, and a handful of distant pin-prick lights marked the town of Algeciras on that war-torn coast. Another handful of lights, much closer, showed where the *Llandnno Chief* yet lay at anchor, just outside the boomed harbour.

The two men walked along, with no appearance of haste, under the date palms. You would have taken them for a couple who had just stepped out from a dance or party somewhere for a breath of air and a cigarette down here on this open promenade which is called the Bastion. Nor would you have been entirely wrong.

Bunny Manders and his ally, the young American, Dan Westray, had not been long detained by the mountainous Sergeant Mifsud at the police office down on the docks.

It had been a shock to Bunny and Dan when the big sergeant, kicking the shut door, had made his enigmatic remark: "Not so fast, gentlemen—not so fast!" But the sergeant's subsequent questioning had been less alarming than they had feared.

He had wanted to know, first, how it came about that Dan had not rejoined his ship on the last tender. The young American had replied glibly that he had met a friend, Mr. Manders, in the town, and in the subsequent celebration of the meeting had entirely overlooked the time. He added that now, as a consequence of meeting his friend, he did not propose to continue on to England in the *Llandnno Chief*, but to leave her here, and travel on to England by a later ship in company with his friend, Mr. Manders. About his luggage, he was not, Dan had said, bothering. Manders could lend him all he needed, and his things aboard the ship could go on to England, where the shipping people would hold them for him.

The explanation had been unexceptionable. Sergeant Mifsud had been compelled to pass it. He had then asked why they were inquiring for Miss Drusilla Brook.

"She's a friend of mine," Dan said. "I wanted to tell her I wasn't going on in the *Llandnno Chief*, and I wanted her to meet Mr. Manders."

"I see," said Sergeant Mifsud. "Well, you know now that the lady's still ashore. Why should she have remained ashore, do you think, Mr. Westray?"

"No idea," Dan lied cheerfully. "Maybe she'd had some reason to change her mind, too."

Mifsud was not satisfied, they could see that. But having no possible excuse on which to hold them, he must needs let them go. Which he did, though none too affably, after examining their passports and noting Bunny's address and the address at which Dan proposed to stay— the Peak Hotel, in both cases.

The allies returned straight to the hotel.

Their interview with Mifsud had made it plain to both that there had been a tightening-up at the docks, that additional police had been drafted there.

"Take it," Dan said, "in conjunction with the radio call for your friend Bell-Evart, and it's plain enough what's happened. You're right in your guess. Bell-Evart's ducked his watchdog Marius, and skipped—and Marius has gone to the Gib authorities for help in rounding him up again."

This explanation seemed probable to Bunny, for the actual truth of what had occurred—that Marius had been murdered—was unknown to both of them.

It was still unknown to them when, after a council of war in Bunny's room at the hotel, they decided to investigate Chundra's store on their own account.

"Raffles entered it, and, as far as we know," Bunny said, "hasn't come out. Your Miss Brook entered it—and again, as far as we know, she's still there. Obviously, the first move for us to make is a discreet reconnaissance of that Hindu hotbed."

Luck was with them. There was a dance on at the Peak Hotel that night. Bunny and Dan attended it, danced with such ladies as they saw unpartnered, and in due course, like everybody else, strolled out for a breath of air in the moonlit gardens.

Unobtrusively to slide out from the hotel gardens was easy. The hotel was a little way up the side of the Rock, above the level of most of the houses; it looked out over the tree and flower-filled park and parade ground called the Alameda.

Bunny, who had been a few days in Gib and had learned his way about, headed down on to the Bastion, from which they cut up through Irish Town to the alley off Main Street, coming out at the side of Chundra's.

Dan went first over the wall into the backyard of the Hindu store. Bunny, following, was actually on the wall when the headlights of a car flashed into the alley and revealed him.

He dropped down into the backyard, and both waited there tensely in the darkness to see if the man in the car proposed to investigate further.

He did so investigate, dropping straight over the wall into Dan's and Bunny's arms; and the allies did the only possible thing. They knocked him cold, abandoned their planned reconnaissance of Chundra's, and bolted.

Now, here they were, out again on the Bastion, heading back for the hotel.

The dance, probably, would not yet be over. The idea in Bunny's mind was that they should slip back unseen into the hotel gardens, re-enter the hotel, dance one or two more numbers. No one would be likely to think, then, that they had ever gone out of the gardens at all.

It had become, now, supremely important that no one at the hotel should suspect their absence. For an entirely new, deadly dangerous factor had entered into the situation. Dan didn't know it, but Bunny did. In the second when he had flashed his torch into the face of the intruder in Chundra's backyard, Bunny had had the worst shock of his life. He had recognised Blake, the criminologist!

Blake, that astute manhunter who months before had come within an ace of bringing about Raffles' arrest and indictment, and who with ironic courtesy had clearly told Raffles that he intended sooner or later to get him— Blake, of all living people, was in Gibraltar!

This was the worst news yet.

Bunny looked up at the vast Rock, towering above them in the moonlight, shouldering the night sky, dwarfing the tiers of crowded buildings that clung to its lower slopes— the Rock of Gibraltar, formidable, majestic, bristling with armaments—and cursed it blackly in his heart. What earthly chance had Raffles, a lone wolf, a hunted man, hemmed in from every side on this restricted, unique mountain, with the arch-enemy, Blake, relentlessly seeking him?

Why was Blake here? How had he got here? Was it possible that during all those months of Raffles' absence in America, Hawaii and Australia, Blake had kept watch on him, Bunny, peacefully writing his book in the Albany chambers in London? Was it possible that Blake had heard of Raffles' arrest in Australia, knew the ship by which he was being brought back, had taken note of Bunny's departure for Gibraltar, and, suspecting that it might be the first step in an attempt to engineer Raffles' escape, had followed him, Bunny, to Gibraltar with intent to checkmate any such scheme?

It seemed damnably likely.

And he was, Bunny reflected, totally in the dark as to what it was all about. He did not even know the charge on which Raffles had been arrested in Melbourne. He knew only that his partner confidently expected a ten-year sentence if he were brought to trial.

How had Raffles contrived to escape his gaoler Marius? Why had he entered Chundra's? Why had he not emerged? Was he still there? Was Blake, even now, searching the Hindu store for Raffles? If Blake did not know Raffles was in that store somewhere, what possible reason had brought the detective to the alley, at that hour, in that way?

Had he, Bunny, made a mis-step in bolting from that backyard? Ought he rather, leaving Blake stunned there, to have hammered at the door of Chundra's, demanded to see Raffles, warned him to get out, Blake was after him?

Heaven knew—not Bunny Manders!

He was in the dark. He saw no glimmer of light anywhere. Even Dan Westray, his new ally, was an enigma. He did not know how far he could trust Dan. The business of Dan, who wanted no truck with the police, and of Drusilla Brook, the American girl who had vanished—as Raffles had vanished—in Chundra's store, made no sense to Bunny.

Of one thing only was he certain: whilst he had seen and recognised Blake in Chundra's backyard, Blake could not possibly have seen him, Bunny. The reconnaissance of Chundra's had failed. Blake, blast him, had intervened. But if they could contrive to slip back unseen into the hotel gardens, Bunny consoled himself, then at least Blake would have nothing on him and Dan.

They had by now, walking quickly, crossed the Alameda. A steep road, arched over by the boughs of tall, red-trunked pines, curved up steeply before them. The hotel was still out of sight, some two hundred yards higher up, round the curve. The moon, through the arching boughs checkered the road with light and dense shadow.

The whine of a car, above the bend, but coming down toward them, jerked Bunny from his preoccupation. The car's headlights silvered the pine trunks, far up the road. Bunny touched Dan's arm.

"Duck for it!"

Hurriedly, the two men climbed the bank to the left, crouched down among the azaleas. The car, containing two naval officers and three girls, all hilarious, shot by.

In the darkness and quiet which followed its passing, Bunny said softly:

"The crowd's breaking up. Hurry! We'll just about make it."

They climbed on up the bank. Along the top of it grew a hedge of prickly pear cactus, inconveniently dense and lavishly needled. Not without a few profane kicks against the pricks, the two found a way through it, and were back once more in the hotel gardens.

Five minutes later, they sauntered leisurely, smoking into the glow of light from the long stone terrace of the hotel. There were still a good many people there, sitting at small tables, chattering; through open french windows, Bunny saw dancing couples, still at it, and heard music.

The two walked up on to the terrace, stood on the threshhold of the french windows, watching the dancers. The crowd had thinned out, but there was still a fairish number left. Bunny felt for his monocle.

He did not find it. He looked down, raised the broken cord in his hand, stared at it for a second, unbelievingly, gave a sudden exclamation.

"Something wrong?" Dan asked.

Bunny detached the cord from his lapel, put it in his pocket.

"Dance," he said.

They found partners and danced. Bunny's partner was a vivacious attractive brunette—a Colonel's daughter. She might have been a sack of potatoes for all Bunny knew. His mind was going step by step over the expedition to Chundra's. Just when had he lost that blasted eyeglass? It was important to know.

By the end of the dance, he was tolerably certain that he could only have lost it in the scuffle in Chundra's backyard. Worse and worse! If Blake had found it, you could trust him to put two and two together. He'd know at once who had been his assailant in that backyard. He'd be up here at the hotel at any minute, wanting to know what Bunny had been after in Chundra's yard. He was a hard man to lie to—and just how good a liar, Bunny wondered, was Dan Westray under pressure?

The dance finished.

"That was quite an experience," said the brunette scathingly. "Now I know what it's like to dance with a spectre. If I were you, I'd haunt my way off to bed before my knees gave away!"

Bunny mumbled an apology. He collected Dan, and they went upstairs together. If that infernal eyeglass should bring Blake snooping up here, it was important that they should decide on their story and get it pat.

That wasn't so easy. Dan wanted to find Drusilla. For some reason, he wanted nothing to do with the police. But when he found himself definitely mixed up with the police, and getting deeper, would he stand the gaff? Or would he come out with the truth?

Bunny didn't know. He had been virtually forced into this alliance with the young American, but Dan was an uncertain ally. You couldn't blame him if he put the skids under the entente when he realised just what sort of fire he was playing with.

But before Blake came, Bunny had to know just where he stood with Dan. That was vital.

"We've got to talk things over, old boy," he said.

"Don't I know it?" Dan said grimly.

No, Bunny thought, you don't—not by a long sight! But he kept the thought to himself.

"We'll go into my room," Dan said.

Bunny had got him a room next to his own on the first floor. Dan opened the door. The room was dark, but through the slats of the closed shutters thin lines of moonlight penetrated. Dan reached for the light switch, and, as he did so, a shadow moved darkly across the lines of moonshine filtering through the shutters.

Bunny saw it, every nerve in him shrieked. "Danger!" He hurled his weight against Dan in a violent shoulder charge, staggering him to one side.

Something thudded, plunk, into the wood of the door-jamb, and the shutters of the window swung open. A shadowy figure showed there in the act of scrambling across the sill on to the small balcony.

Bunny lunged forward, past Dan, who had fallen on one knee, and hurled himself on that figure in the window. He got an arm crooked round the man's neck from behind, and, dragging him back from the sill, fell with him, rolled over on top of him, ground his knee into the man's chest, and his thumbs into the man's throat, stranglingly.

"Lie still!"

The lights blazed on as Dan got to the switch. He closed the door, strode across and swung the shutters together.

Only then did Bunny take his hands from the man's throat, and, whipping a small automatic from his hip-pocket, rose. He covered the prone figure.

"You can get up now!"

Dan was staring at the small, heavy, horn-handled knife embedded inches deep in the door-jamb, the hilt still slightly quivering. The young American was pale under his tan; sweat gleamed on his forehead. He spoke hoarsely:

"I guess that was meant for me!"

"You guess right," Bunny said. Few people would have recognised in his harsh, deadly tone the usually lazy, cool, faintly drawling voice of Bunny Manders. He addressed the man on the floor. "Get up, you—get up before I boot you up!"

The man struggled to a sitting position, coughing, fingering his throat. He was a thin, swarthy individual, in a washed-out, blue linen suit, a beret, rope-soled shoes without socks.

"I've seen you before," Bunny said, and abruptly snapped the fingers of his free hand. "I remember! You're one of those hombres who pester round peddling crayfish. How did you get in here?"

The man did not answer. He sat on the floor sullenly, a hand at his throat.

"That's easy," Dan said. "He came up the vine under my balcony. This room's at the side of the hotel. I guess he's just a second-storey sneak-thief. We barged in on him, and he lost his head."

"It won't wash," Bunny said. "He might have tried a dash for it, but he wouldn't have thrown that knife. He was waiting for you, Dan; he was laying for you, and we're going to know why! Hear that, hombre? We're going to know why!"

"No comprendo!"

"No?" said Bunny. "Well, we'll talk Spanish. Hablamos Espanol, sabe?" He went on, in Spanish: "Are you going to talk without trouble, or have we got to knock it out of you? Think quick!"

The man abandoned the pretence that he knew no English; spoke, in that tongue, with a flash of defiance:

"You can do nothing. Nada, nada! You dare not call the police!"

Bunny said dangerously:

"That's just about what I wanted to hear from you, hombre! Hear that, Dan? He knows we dare not call the police. If he knows that much about us, he knows a deuce of a lot more. D'you still think he was here by chance— just a sneak-thief—and not here because he'd specifically found out your room and for some reason was laying for you?"

"It looks that way."

"And it's the way it looks," said Bunny Manders. "And he's not going to talk; the hombre's not going to tell us why he was laying for you. So he thinks!" His smile was iron. "Open the bathroom door there, Dan. Turn the taps on, and leave it open. The water'll cover the noise when he starts to yell. Then yank that knife out of the door-jamb there, give it to me, and come and sit on our visitor's bean. I'm going," Bunny said, with icy ferocity, "to carve patterns in this hombre's hide till he changes his mind and talks, and talks fast!"

CHAPTER 11

THREE-THOUSAND-AND-ONE LOST SOULS

FROM in front of the police station, Blake had seen, far away to the left and high up, the reflected glow of the searchlight, over on the other side of the Rock, which had smashed Raffles' attempt, engineered by Lal Chundra, to escape from Gibraltar.

Blake had not connected the searchlight with the case in hand.

Further, Blake and Tinker had both heard and seen the military ambulance which, with clanging alarm bell, had swept down Main Street shortly after the flashing of that searchlight.

Blake had not connected the ambulance, either, with the case in hand. There was no reason why he should. He did not know where Raffles was.

Actually, that ambulance was answering a telephone call from the guard-house at the British Gate. It was on its way, when Blake and Tinker saw it, to pick up a sentry who had been seriously wounded while patrolling the beach immediately behind the Hindu burning-ghats, out between the racecourse and Catalan Bay.

Raffles heard the ambulance approaching the burning-ghats; the wild clangour of its bell startled the night; its headlights swept blazing along the road between the racecourse and the towering precipice, the face of stone, which Gibraltar here presents to Spain.

Raffles wondered if that Tommy, whose life he had tried to save, were seriously wounded, or dead.

It would be to fetch that Tommy, Raffles guessed, that the ambulance was on its way; and when the clangour of the bell ceased, as the ambulance pulled up near the burning-ghats, his guess was confirmed.

Between the burning-ghats and the racecourse, there was a long, narrow strip of waste land. It was flat and sandy, but the wind had blown the sand into low waves, forming rounded ridges and shallow depressions. The tussocks of tough dune-grass were burnt, blackened, with an acrid smell.

Following his escape from the beach, his climb over the wall into the burning-ghats, Raffles had run swiftly round that wall on the inside, and climbed out of the ghats on the side farthest from the beach.

He now lay in a depression on this strip of sandy waste land, getting his breath and his bearings.

The sheer, towering precipice, from the foot of which the land stretched away as flat as a billiard table, cast its deep shadow as far as the British boundary, so that his position out here was at least not complicated by moonlight. Away to his left, however, the searchlight still stabbed down from the Rock; its shaft was motionless; its brilliant eye was fixed steadily upon that part of the beach where the Hindus had fallen foul of the military sentries.

With the fear that the searchlight might presently come questing round over this bit of waste land, Raffles had chosen for concealment a sandy depression that was partly masked by cactus growths. The searchlight, he calculated, could pass right over him now without revealing to those alert eyes up there in the galleries which honeycombed the precipice.

That was all right as far as it went, but what was to be his next move?

Some two hundred and fifty yards behind him, there out straight across this neck of flat land, which stretched away from the foot of the precipice, the British fence. It was a high fence, entangled with barbed wire, alarm wires, and probably electrified, and it was patrolled by sentries. Beyond it was the treeless, bushless strip of neutral territory, with the Atlantic on one side and the Mediterranean on the other, which separated British territory from Spanish.

But his chances of getting through the British fence, let alone of crossing the shelterless neutral territory and of getting through the Spanish fence and guards, were exactly nil.

Raffles ruled out the possibility.

Here he was, crouched in a hole in the ground, with defences on every side of him far stronger than those which surround a prison. He had not even a weapon.

He was a criminal. He had committed many crimes and escaped unpunished. Yet he was hard-pressed now as he had never been hard-pressed in his life, and he was innocent of the two crimes which had brought him to this pass. If taken, he would be sentenced for the Forge Park robbery—and he had not robbed Forge Park; or he would hang for the murder of Marius—and he had not murdered Marius.

Raffles thought, with a certain sardonic humour, that this was a pretty fair example of retribution.

Ninety-nine men out of a hundred, placed as he was, would have given themselves up. But Raffles—he, A. J. Raffles, by gum—was the hundredth man! They wanted him? Then let 'em take him! He'd give them a run for their money. He was the hare, they were the hounds—and, by Heaven, they'd get a full course!

It was at this stage that he heard the ambulance bell clanging in the night, saw its headlights race along the road under the precipice, heard it draw up before the burning-ghats, away to his left.

He hoped that that Tommy hadn't been killed. Queer to think that if he'd let that Hindu throw his knife, he, Raffles, might have been at sea now—safe; or, anyway, a long sight safer than he was at this minute. It had been, he supposed, quixotic—if not definitely daft—to try to save the life of that unknown Cockney private at the expense of his own freedom. If he hadn't smacked down that Hindu, the Tommy would have had a knife in him before he had a chance to fire his rifle; if he hadn't fired his rifle, the alarm would not have gone up, and Raffles at this minute would be en route to Oran.

Still, he didn't regret what he'd done, though he regretted—and how!—this jam it had got him into.

Well—to blazes with that! The dice were loaded against him, but surely there must be some advantage on his side.

He considered. First, he no longer fulfilled in any particular the radio description of "Major Alan Bell-Evart". His clothes were different, his skin was darkened, his hair was plastered, he wore tinted glasses—he was Rabaji Ram Dass, Hindu. (Disadvantage: If anybody addressed him in Hindustani, he was sunk!)

Second advantage: Bunny was in Gib. If he could get in touch with Bunny, something might be done.

Third advantage: Gibraltar was packed with strangers, refugees.

Refugees!

Raffles rolled over in his depression in the sand—this reminded him of the war and of a shell hole in which he had once spent some tense hours—and peered across toward the racecourse. All dark over there, but in that vast, flat circle, he knew, there were camped some three thousand refugees. They would be mostly strangers to each other, of course; there was bound to be a certain amount of confusion; they were all wrapped up in their own troubles.

Here, he thought, was a chance of, at any rate, temporary shelter. Ram Dass, refugee merchant from Seville——

He chose Seville because he knew that there were a good many Hindu traders in that town.

Five minutes later, Raffles was crouched in darkness under the fence which surrounded the racecourse. It was a rail fence. Just inside it was a belt of eucalyptus trees, their scent pungent on the sultry air.

Raffles ducked between the rails of the fence, weaved his way cautiously between the belt of trees to the inside edge. To his left were the stands, saddling enclosure, stables, and tote building, looming shadowy. All was quiet. Nearby he could make out the vague, white shapes of Army bell-tents; and here and there across the wide expanse of the racecourse, the spark of campfires and of naphtha lanterns showed other tents. The racecourse was become a small town of tents—a canvas town of the homeless and unfortunate, to whom Britain, following her old tradition, had opened her gates.

Ghost-like, between the rows of tents, avoiding the dying campfires and the naphtha lanterns, stole a shadowy figure.

Presently it disappeared.

Low-voiced, but peremptory orders, and the thud of grounded rifle-butts over near the racecourse buildings as the guard was changed; the clang of an ambulance bell speeding by toward the town and the Military Hospital—these alone were the sounds that disturbed the peace of the camp of unfortunates as the moon sank to its setting, a deeper darkness closed over the impending Rock, and the dawn wind blew fresh out of the east.

Of all those three thousand—and one—lost souls in the refugee encampment, none bore a more virulent hatred for General Francisco Franco than Emilio Roca. Emilio Roca was by profession a barber; his small shop, with its bead-curtained doorway, had stood until recently on the waterfront of Algeciras, facing Gibraltar across the bay. It no longer stood there. Early in the Civil War a shell from the Franco cruiser, *Canarias*, had rendered it a heap of rubble. The same shell had mangled beyond recognition the two British-made, nickel-plated, adjustable barber-chairs, of extreme elegance, which were the pride of Emilio Roca's life, the tangible evidence of his ambition, and the repository of ten years' savings.

Never so long as he lived would Emilio Roca forgive the destruction of his incomparable barber-chairs. He was thirty years of age, and, because he had saved every centimo in order to purchase those chairs, marriage had been beyond his means. He was still a bachelor. His chairs had been everything to him, and they had been destroyed. Revenge remained as the sole object of his life.

He fought with the rabble which retreated from Algeciras when Franco's Moorish regulares entered the town. In the brief but bitter fighting in the sun-scorched cork woods above the town he killed five Moors with an old-fashioned hammer sporting-rifle which had belonged to his father. He counted the five dead Moors as scarcely the beginning of the revenge he intended to wreak for the destruction of his chairs. He fought furiously in the last stand of the rabble before La Linea, was wounded, and with the collapse of the defence escaped across the frontier into Gibraltar.

There he remained, convalescing from his wounds, while the Franco juggernaut crushed along the coast, took Estepona and Marbella, and after meeting stubborn resistance, at last overwhelmed Malaga. There in Gibraltar, Emilio Roca remained, dreaming of finding a rifle again in his hands, hoping against hope to find himself in the next bunch of refugees which the British, faced with dire overcrowding, shipped to Valencia.

Such was Emilio Roca; such was his story.

Roca occupied a tent near the centre of the racecourse. He shared it with four others, all men. It was not a bell-tent; bell-tents were scarce; such as there were had been reserved for women and children. Roca's tent was made out of old barrel-hoops, stuck in the parched, iron-hard ground and covered with an ancient tarpaulin bearing the British War Office stamp. It was open on one side; the men lay in a row, their rope-sandalled feet toward the open side.

The first of the dawn bugles, ringing out thin and far as the Union Jack went up over the Rock, awakened Emilio Roca from a dream of battle and revenge. He threw back the dingy blanket which covered him, and sat up. He was a small man, lean, hard and wiry, with a thin, dark face, extraordinarily lined for a man of thirty, and black, hot eyes. He wore dungarees, a once-white shirt, and frayed-out, rope-soled sandals; these were all the clothes he possessed, except for a beret, which he now took from under the old leather cushion he used as a pillow, and pulled aslant on his head. He also took from under the cushion a packet of coarse tobacco and some cigarette papers.

He rolled and lighted a cigarette, yawned, glanced at his sleeping companions, and sat up straighter, staring.

There were not four others in the tent, there were five.

The fifth was at the far end of the row. He lay on his back on the bare ground; he had no blanket. He wore a black suit, and a white shirt with a narrow black tie; he had the coffee-dark skin, the jet-black, plastered hair of a Hindu, and wore tinted spectacles.

Emilio Roca shook the shoulder of the man next him, and when the man sat up, yawning and stretching, indicated the stranger.

"Quien es?"

The man shook his head.

"No se. Un Indio. He entered our tent late in mistake for his own, tal vez. I didn't hear him."

The others hadn't heard him, either. Waking one by one, they discussed the Hindu, while Emilio Roca broke bits of charcoal into a small brazier outside the tent, lighted a fire, and went to work frying bunuelos.

The rays of the sun, now lifting its red disc above the horizon on the Mediterranean side, struck slanting across the camp on the racecourse. The sheer, grey stone precipice of the Rock seemed to hang suspended over the camp. The sea on the Mediterranean side, alight with the sunrise, was empty; on the other, the Atlantic side, the shadow of the Rock still lay over the bay. There, beyond the network of masts and rigging in the boomed harbour, the white tourist ship, the *Llandnno Chief*, still lay at anchor outside the booms. The small figures of her crew were visible, swabbing decks.

A white-canopied horse-carriage, with four policemen in it going off duty, clip-clopped along the road at the foot of the precipice; a fatigue party, in working uniforms with picks and shovels over their shoulders, tramped by, whistling.

All over the racecourse, usually the rendezvous of the smart set—the garrison officers and their ladies, and the well-to-do Gibraltar business people—the camp was stirring. Ragged, dark-skinned children played among the tents; towsled women, some with babies at their breasts, squatted over pans of frying bunuelos; tattered men emerged, yawning and scratching, to blink at the day and roll cigarettes. The by-products of civil war—the flotsam and jetsam——

It was still cool, but the unclouded brassiness of the sky eastward promised a blazing day.

These bunuelos the refugees were frying are made out of batter; they taste like doughnuts, and are the common breakfast of the poor Spanish. The ingredients for them, together with a coffee that was mostly chicory, the British had made a ration issue to the refugees.

Raffles woke to the aroma of the bunuelos frying in Roca's pan. He was puzzled for a second. The light particularly puzzled him—till, putting a hand to his eyes, he realised that he wore tinted glasses. Then in a flash he remembered everything. He was in the tent which, after glancing into half-a-dozen others—he had chosen because it contained only men, and had space for another. He sat up.

Emilio Roca, squatted over his frying-pan, glanced at him, and nodded.

"Salud!"

The word gave Raffles his cue. Salud was the word for greeting and parting which, on the Popular Front side, had displaced the Buenos Dias and Adios of the old Spain.

"Salud," Raffles said, and raised a clenched fist in the salute of the People's Front.

Thereby he earned at once the approval of Emilio Roca and his tent-mates.

Speaking fair Spanish, Raffles apologised for his intrusion overnight. His name, he explained, was Rabaji Ram Dass—of Seville. After a long period of hiding, he had at last got through Nationalist territory to Gibraltar. He had been admitted late overnight to the encampment and told to doss where he could find space.

Roca accepted the explanation without question; that clenched fist salute of Ram Dass' had rubbed him up the right way.

"Quiere comer, companero?"

Raffles accepted with gratitude this invitation to eat. He had not, he said, eaten since yesterday morning— which was the truth. The greasy, doughnut-like bunuelo tasted better than many an Entrecote Mirabeau he had eaten at the Ritz; in swank hotels he had sampled worse coffee than this watery-brown, hot, faintly iodine-flavoured liquid. There was plenty of it, and plenty of bunuelo.

As he ate, squatting before the tent on the parched, yellow grass, there rose in him a feeling of elation. True, the overnight attempt to get out of Gib had failed, but here it was, morning, and he was still at large. He'd beat the game yet——

He borrowed the "makings" from Roca, rolled a cigarette, sat talking to his hosts. Skilfully he pumped them for details of the running of the camp. He learned that the camp was under heavy guard of military and police; a permit was necessary to leave it, and a permit was hard to get.

"But I know a way to get out," said Roca. "Every day I slip out, I go up town, get odd jobs—portering in the market, holding horses, anything—to make a few pesetas. Every centimo I shall need when los Ingleses ship me to Valencia."

Raffles became conscious of his heart, thumping slow and heavy; he was glad the tinted glasses hid his eyes.

"They'll send you to Valencia, will they?"

"Two or three times a week," said Roca, "los Ingleses send a batch of refugees back to our own country—by destroyer to Valencia. If they did not"—he shrugged—"we should eat them out of house and home. Even as it is, they are short of food on the Rock, and they fear epidemic among us from overcrowding."

"How do they decide," Raffles asked, keeping a sudden taut excitement out of his voice, "who goes and who stays?"

"No se," said Roca. "An officer comes to inspect. He decides. You will see. He will be here soon. We must clean the tent before he comes. Los Ingleses, they are tediously particular; every blanket, it must be folded."

Now for the showdown, Raffles thought. Would this British officer be on the lookout for a stray Hindu in this camp of three thousand refugees, who were bound to have among them a scattering of many nationalities, many shades of colour? It depended on whether any of Lal Chundra's men had been taken alive last night; whether, if taken, they had blown the gaff on "Ram Dass".

This inspection was going to be dangerous. But it had to be faced.

This business, too, of batches of refugees being shipped to Valencia. Was there a glimmer of hope there? By heaven, it'd be funny if "Ram Dass" could manage to attach himself to an outgoing batch—and, under the noses of the unsuspecting police, be shipped in a British destroyer to Valencia!

"The officer comes," said Roca.

The sun was now well up. Already the heat blur trembled between the tents. A small group of very official appearance was working its way slowly from tent to tent—a young British captain, in light khaki tunic and riding-breeches, his Sam Brown belt and his riding-boots polished to parade-ground brilliance; two English nurses, in starched caps and aprons, from the military hospital; an R.A.M.C. sergeant, and a young Gibraltar police-inspector in uniform. The latter was Inspector Parodi, though Raffles didn't know it.

He rose, with Roca and the others, as the group approached. The R.A.M.C. sergeant looked into the tent, while the young captain ran his eye over the six men.

Every nerve in Raffles' body was strung taut.

But the captain's glance remained entirely casual until it reached Emilio Roca.

"Ah, this is the chap who talks so much about wanting to be sent to Valencia. Well, tell him he's going on the destroyer Wild Swan tomorrow, inspector—and a good riddance to him!"

Inspector Parodi translated, and Emilio Roca exploded into a tirade of excited gratitude.

The little group moved on. Through the tinted glasses of "Ram Dass", Raffles looked after it. He had got through his ordeal. So far, so good. But it was not so much relief he felt as an intense excitement.

So the destroyer *Wild Swan* was leaving tomorrow for Valencia with a batch of refugees! Was it, indeed?

He borrowed the "makings" from Emilio Roca, rolled and lighted a cigarette, motioned the lean, dark, hot-eyed little man into the shelter of the tent.

"Amigo," he said, "I envy you. You are to go to Valencia. You will rejoin the militia. You will be able again to strike a blow. Por Dios, it may be weeks, months, before my turn comes."

"Lo siento——" Roca began, but the "Hindu" interrupted him.

"I have money. Look!" He took a wallet from his pocket. It was fat with English banknotes. "Tell me— what would fifty pounds, esterlina, be worth in Valencia?"

"A fortune!"

Roca's eyes glowed.

The spaniard and the "Hindu" sat close together in the low, makeshift tent.

"Help me," the "Hindu" said softly, "and I pay you fifty pounds. I, too, wish to travel in the destroyer tomorrow. Tell me, there are other men of my race, other Indios, in the camp?"

"But, yes." Roca spread his hands. "Twenty, perhaps. Thirty. Hindu traders who have settled in Spain to work the tourist traffic, and become naturalized. Now, with the war, they are like we Spaniards—dispossessed, refugees."

"It is even so with me," said "Ram Dass". "And it may be that among these twenty or thirty Indios there are several, perhaps, who are to leave on the *Wild Swan*. Now, you have been some time here: you know the camp and its ways. You could approach these Indios discreetly—find out if there are any among them who are booked to leave on the British destroyer? I would pay you."

He took a ten-pound note from his wallet, gave it to Roca.

"If you help me, there will be more."

Roca placed the note carefully in a pocket in the broad leather belt he wore buckled tight outside his dungarees. His eyes glittered.

"Companero, trust me!"

"Another thing," said Raffles. "Today I must somehow enter the town. You say you know a way of getting out of the camp without a permit——"

"It is simple, companero. You see, there, the belt of eucalyptus trees?"

Raffles nodded. It was the belt of trees through which he had entered the racecourse camp overnight.

"To the right of them," Roca said, "is the road. Across the road there are men at work, building petrol storage tanks. The driver of one of the lorries, he is a British subject now; but once he was of Algeciras, across the bay, and he is a friend of mine. Presently I show you how we work it."

Accordingly, when they were sure that the camp inspection was over, Emilio Roca and his "Hindu" friend sauntered between the crowded tents towards the belt of eucalyptus trees. Reaching them, they sat down in the shade, close to the rails that ran round the racecourse. Beyond the rails was that strip of sandy wasteland where Raffles had hidden overnight; across the wasteland was the white wall, peeling in the intense sun-glare, of the burning-ghats.

The road ran along to the right of where the two men sat. Across the road stood the steel girders of a building in course of construction, right up against the foot of the precipice. Men were at work there; a derrick was clattering, heaving blocks of concrete into position.

Patrolling the road, from which they could watch the rails of the racecourse and the sandy wasteland outside it, were two sentries in the light khaki tunics, pith helmets and tartan slacks of a Scottish regiment. They carried fixed bayonets on their rifles.

Raffles' heart sank.

"Espera, espera," Roca said confidently—"wait!"

Partly masked by the trees from observation from the camp itself, the two men sat casually smoking. You would have judged that they had chosen the spot solely for its shade. When they had been there about half an hour a heavy Thorneycroft lorry, stacked with steel girders, came clanking along the road. The lorry pulled up in front of the building job. As the driver descended from his seat he glanced casually towards the racecourse rails.

Roca pulled off his beret.

The unloading of the lorry took about half an hour, when the driver hooked up the backboard again, swung the starting-handle, climbed back into his seat. To turn the lorry round, he engaged reverse gear and backed the ponderous vehicle off the road on to the sand wasteland, keeping close to the rails of the racecourse.

Raffles saw the tail of the lorry, backing towards him—and understood.

"Go!" breathed Emilio Roca.

The lorry, entirely blocking the view of the sentries, backed to within a few yards of where the men sat, inside the racecourse rails.

Raffles leaped to his feet, ducked through the rails, caught the tailboard of the lorry, pulled himself over it, threw himself flat on the floorboards.

The lorry, starting forward with a jerk as first gear was engaged, curved out past the sentries and clattered away along the dusty, sun-smitten road between the racecourse and the looming precipice.

CHAPTER 12

THE ITALIAN MAIL

DIRECTLY to enter Main Street you must pass under the old, grey arch of the Water Gate. This opens off from a species of square formed by the high, enormously thick, grey walls of the ancient casemates. In the centre of this square there stands a clock tower, surrounded by granite watering-troughs, about which at all hours of the day are ranked a dozen or more of Gibraltar's characteristic, top-heavy, white-canopied horse-carriages.

So high are the walls of the casemates that to be in the square is to feel as though you were on the bed of a moat, and so thick are the walls that here and there in them, at ground levels, are square, dark openings, like caverns, and these are cabmen's eating-houses, workmen's cafes, cheap tobacco stores, actually hollowed out of the concrete casemates.

The heat and glare in this hemmed-in, airless, moat-like plaza is formidable. The horses droop in their shafts. Over the radiators of parked cars quivers a visible, almost crackling heat-blur. The cocheros and taxi-drivers shelter like troglodytes in those black caverns in the casemate walls.

Before one such cavern there clattered to a standstill the huge Thorneycroft lorry which was engaged in hauling girders from the docks to the construction job out near the racecourse. The driver switched off his engine, looked back through the small square opening in the back of the cab.

"Esta bien, Emilio."

Through the opening snaked a lean, coffee-coloured hand, holding a one-pound Bank of Gibraltar note.

"For you, friend," said a voice in Spanish. "I am not Emilio. I am a friend of his. Tell me, what's this hole in the wall you've stopped at?"

"The Cafe Obrero," said the lorry driver, took the banknote, and added: "Any friend of Emilio Roca's is a friend of mine."

The face of a Hindu, wearing tinted glasses, looked at him through the little square opening, and the Hindu smiled with a flash of white teeth. "Thank you, friend. It has a telephone, the Cafe Obrero?"

The driver nodded.

"Thank you," said the Hindu again. "Salud, friend."

"Salud!"

The Hindu climbed over the side of the lorry, dropped to the ground—in the murderous heat the very tarmac was sticky under his shoes—and, as the lorry trundled away, walked into that low, square opening in the casemate wall.

After the glare of the sunshine outside, the darkness within seemed as black almost as that of night. It was a hot, sticky darkness, heavy with the smells of garlic, chicory, coarse tobacco and human sweat.

Raffles paused, cursing the tinted glasses of "Ram Dass", which aggravated the darkness. It was some moments before his eyes began to grow accustomed to the gloom, and he saw that he was in a sort of rectangular tunnel, along each wall of which was placed a line of small tables.

Cabmen lounged at the tables—ragged, dark-skinned hombres, eating, drinking, arguing over dominoes, draughts, poker dice. From the roof hung hams, long salami sausages, wrapped in mutton-cloth or silver paper, strings of garlic and onions, and behind a counter on the left—a counter stacked with bottles and glasses and bearing a huge coffee-urn—stood a fat, opulently moustached man, staring curiously at Raffles.

Raffles stepped forward to the counter, bought a box of fifty Player's—one-and-six—ordered a bottle of wine, a loaf, ham and olives, and asked to use the telephone. He spoke in the babu English of the Gibraltar Hindu.

The fat waiter-proprietor led him right down the tunnel to its far end, indicated the telephone which stood on a shelf against the wall. He snapped on an electric bulb over the 'phone, and, indicating a table nearby, said: "I bring your food here."

He shuffled off. Raffles seized the telephone-book which hung against the wall on a nail, skimmed it through till he reached the Classified Hotel section. He ran his finger down the list. At which hotel was Bunny most likely to be staying? At a guess, the Rock Hotel.

He rang the Rock, in his babu English asked for "Meestaire Mandaire", was told that no such name was on the Rock Hotel register, rang the Hotel Bristol, and was again disappointed. This was worrying. Bunny might be using an alias. He rang the third most likely hotel—the Peak. A girl's voice answered:

"Mr. Manders? One moment. I'll find out if he's in."

Raffles, waiting, drew deeply on his cigarette, filling his lungs with the good Virginia smoke, and glanced round to see if anyone was near him. But only the tables at the far end, near the square of sunshine which marked the entrance, were occupied. Abruptly a voice spoke in his ear:

"Hallo? Mr. Manders speaking."

"Ah, Meestaire Mandaire," Raffles said, speaking softly, cupping a hand about his mouth. "The leather pouffes you purchase, we have deliver them to the Cafe Obrero, opposite Water Gate, nearby docks. It will be easee to pick them up there on your way to ship."

There was a second's pause. Then Bunny's voice said coolly: "Good. Thank you. The pouffes are all right?"

"Oah, assuredlee, meestaire—in veree perfect condition."

"I'm glad to hear it. Good-bye."

"A veree good day to you, distinguished Meestaire," said "Rabaji Ram Dass", and hung up with a quiet chuckle in the voice of A. J. Raffles.

Good old Bunny! He was quick in the uptake; he had plenty of gumption. He'd be along soon.

Raffles sat down to tackle ravenously the wine, bread, ham and olives with which the fat waiter-proprietor was approaching the table near the telephone.

"Past noon," Raffles thought, as he poured himself a glass of wine, "—past noon, and I'm still at large. I have a plan of escape, and I'm in touch with Bunny. By the Lord Harry, I'll beat the rap yet!"

And, less than half a mile away, Blake of Baker Street, in that same moment, was thinking much the same thing.

"Past noon," Blake thought, "and Raffles still at large! Now, what's the answer?"

The criminologist, too, was at lunch. He was lunching in the Cafe Universal—that cafe which so conveniently faced the Hindu store of Chundra, Khitagara & Co. across Main Street.

The radio was blaring music across the dim, cool cafe. Blake poured himself a glass of wine. As he did so the music ceased, the voice of the announcer stated:

"Here, again, is the description of Major Alan Bell-Evart. Height——" The description continued. "Any person," finished the announcer, "having information as to the whereabouts of Major Bell-Evart should communicate at once with Inspector"—there was a second's pause—"with Inspector Parodi at police headquarters."

Captain Kerry Adam, who was lunching with Blake, looked grimly at the criminologist.

"You can't hush things up in this town. There's been no official announcement, but everybody in the Rock knows of the murders of Marius and Sacarello!"

Blake held up his wineglass to the light. But it was not at the colour of the wine that the grey, deep-set eyes of the criminologist looked. It was at the Hindu store across the sun-smitten, crowded street. Blake had not by mere chance chosen the Cafe Universal for lunch. Like Bunny Manders, the day before, he had noted the excellence of this cafe as a post from which to observe Chundra's. Actually, he and the Army sleuth were at the same table in the window as Bunny had occupied yesterday.

Blake had come a long way in the case since his scuffle with the two prowlers in the backyard of that store across the street.

In the form of a bandage about the palm of his right hand, and a bruise on his right cheekbone, he bore the outward marks of that scuffle. But the information he had gleaned from it was cheap at the price of a few trifling cuts and a bruise. The monocle had told him much. On his return to police headquarters—to which he had gone immediately after knocking up and closely questioning the proprietor and waiter of the Bar Monte Cristo, where Marius had died—he had sent for the police officer in charge of passport records.

This was the mountainous Sergeant Mifsud.

Examination of the passport sheets, which Mifsud brought up from the police office on the docks, quickly revealed the name of Manders, proving that the monocle had not lied!

The discovery of the name of Raffles' partner, and of the fact that Manders had arrived in Gibraltar some days before the *Llandnno Chief*, bringing Raffles as a prisoner, was due, occasioned Blake a certain grim satisfaction. It threw light upon dark places. Beyond question now Bell-Evart was an alias for A. J. Raffles. Manders, of course, had come to Gibraltar with some scheme for engineering Raffles' escape.

But here Sergeant Mifsud, seeing which name interested Blake on that foolscap sheet of passport details, advanced some further information. He told Blake of Manders' visit, with Dan Westray, Jr., to the dock police office, and of their inquiry after the American girl, Drusilla Brook.

To Blake, this was a puzzling complication. If a straight plan to engineer Raffles' escape had brought Manders to Gibraltar, what was behind this business of the young Americans, Dan Westray and Drusilla Brook? Who were they, anyhow?

"You say," Blake asked, "that Manders gave his Gibraltar address as Peak Hotel, and that Westray said he intended to stay at the same place?"

"It is so."

"And this Miss Brook—she's not been checked through as having returned to the ship?"

"No, sir."

"Well, if she's not gone back to the ship, she must be staying on the Rock somewhere. Will you find out where for me, sergeant? I'd like a chat with her."

Mifsud gone, Blake considered the situation. Manders and Westray, who evidently was working with him, would have raced back to their hotel after the scuffle in Chundra's backyard. That, Blake thought, was certain. If he tackled Manders on the point that cool, elegant young man would merely deny ever having been anywhere near the alley. The monocle was suggestive, but it was not proof, and Manders was a level headed liar on occasion, as Blake knew. More was to be gained, the criminologist thought, by putting a discreet "tail" on Manders than by tackling him direct.

Blake knew no more discreet and skilful tail than his own assistant, Tinker. This was a job right down Tinker's street. Blake dispatched him on it.

Left alone, the criminologist sat for some time, in thought, at Inspector Sacarello's desk. The unshaded bulb over his head shone on his high temples, from which his dark, crisp hair was deeply receded, and cast shadows over his tanned, aquiline, handsome face.

The problem that principally exercised his attention was—Chundra's!

Marius had been killed in the Bar Monte Cristo. Sacarello, after his examination of the murder scene, had put seals on the room, but had left no guard on it. The most plausible explanation of the visit of Manders and his unaccountable companion, Westray, to that alley off Main Street was this, that they had some purpose for breaking into that sealed room in the Bar Monte Cristo.

If this were so, then the sound of a car slowing down in Main Street with the evident intention of turning into the alley might have alarmed Manders and Westray before they had effected their entrance into the Bar Monte Cristo. Knowing that the car's headlights would at any second flash down the alley, and with no place to conceal themselves, nothing seemed more probable than that they should have scaled the nearest wall—Chundra's— with the intention of hiding in that backyard. But Blake's headlights had touched one of them in the act of scaling the wall.

There was an explanation of Manders' and Westray's presence in the backyard of Chundra's store. It seemed the only possible one. For, though the thought crossed Blake's mind that it would be in keeping with Raffles' subtlety to choose as his hide-out the building next door to that in which had been committed the murder for which he was "wanted", the detective dismissed the thought. A man who was as subtle as all that would be much too subtle to permit his followers to rendezvous at his actual hideout.

No, the first explanation must be right. Chundra's was not in itself significant. The Bar Monte Cristo had been Manders' and Westray's objective. They had dodged into Chundra's backyard merely to take cover.

Then what were they after at the Bar Monte Cristo?

Blake smoked a lot of pipes over that question. He got nowhere with it. It led up the same blind alley as the point he had raised earlier, to Captain Adam. Raffles must know that motive and circumstantial evidence were together sufficient to hang him for the murder of Marius. The fact that he had bolted proved he knew that. But why, if not to destroy some piece of evidence in the Marius murder, had Inspector Sacarello been killed? And why, if not to destroy some piece of evidence left in the Bar

Monte Cristo, should Manders and Westray have gone to that alley tonight?

The puzzle did not "jell" as it should. Somewhere, Blake felt, he was missing a vital piece of the jigsaw.

Searching for it, his mind seized upon two obvious incongruities. The first was inherent in the character of the man he hunted. Now that he was certain that "Bell-Evart" was an alias, that Raffles was the man he was dealing with, Blake no longer had to guess at the character of his quarry. He knew it from experience. And he would have staked his reputation that Raffles was not a killer—above all, a killer who killed by means of a knife in the back. That was the first incongruity.

The second was this: In questioning the proprietor of the Bar Monte Cristo, he had elicited the fact that for some years Marius had been known there by appearance though not by name. On and off, sometimes once or twice a year, sometimes a dozen times a year, he used the bar. That was odd, Blake thought, for a Yard man. The Yard had very little to do with Gibraltar, as far as he knew.

But this latter incongruity was soon to be explained.

When he returned to police headquarters in the morning, after a few hours' sleep at Captain Adam's bungalow, a cable from the Yard awaited him. Decoded, it read:

GOVERNMENT HOUSE, GIBRALTAR, HAS NOTIFIED US OF SACARELLO MURDER. UNDERSTAND YOU ARE HANDLING INVESTIGATION. GOVERNMENT HOUSE CABLE GIVES US IMPRESSION THEY STILL BELIEVE JAMES CHAYNE MARIUS TO HAVE BEEN YARD OPERATIVE. IN CASE YOU SHOULD NOT HAVE SEEN OUR CABLE TO SACARELLO ON THIS POINT WE REPEAT IT AS FOLLOWS.

And what followed brought Blake to his feet as astoundedly as it had brought Inspector Sacarello, the day before.

James Chayne Marius was an impostor.

In possession at last of this knowledge, which in his view

132

profoundly altered the case, Blake went to visit the captain of the *Llandnno Chief*. From him, the criminologist learned of the charge on which, Marius had told the captain, "Bell-Evart" had been arrested—namely, robbery with violence at Forge Park, Westchester County.

It was with the feeling that at last he was getting somewhere that Blake returned to police headquarters—and to two further startling items of news.

The first came from the massive Sergeant Mifsud. Acting on Blake's instructions, the sergeant had tried every hotel and boarding-house on the Rock in search of the American girl, Drusilla Brook. He had failed to find her.

Blake was startled.

"But that's ridiculous, sergeant! She came ashore yesterday; we know that. And we know she's not returned to the ship. Therefore, she must be on the Rock somewhere."

"If she is," said the swarthy, mountainous sergeant, "then she's in hiding. There's not much sense in any stranger on the Rock trying to pass under a false name, Mr. Blake, because the dock police always has his passport details. But just in case she might have tried it on, I got her description from the *Llandnno Chief*'s purser, and checked every single hotel and boarding-house over again giving her description. She's on the Rock, Mr. Blake, seguramente, but——"

Blake said abruptly:

"It doesn't follow that she's in hiding, sergeant. You overlook the possibility that she may be staying with some private resident. We can't very well conduct a door-to-door canvass, but this American girl must be found. We shall have to bother Gibraltar Radio Station again."

"That means a Government House order, Mr. Blake."

The criminologist scribbled a note.

"Take that to Government House, sergeant."

Blake had little time to consider this new development. Mifsud had not been gone five minutes when a constable knocked on the office door and entered with a cable. It was addressed to Sacarello and marked "Priority". Blake opened it. The cable was from the Sheriff of Westchester County, N.Y., and was in International Police Code. Worked out, it read:

YOUR CABLE TO HAND. NO ROBBERY WAS COMMITTED AT ANDREW PAYNE HULBURD ESTATE, FORGE PARK, ON NIGHT OF JANUARY FIFTEENTH. MR. HULBURD IS AT PRESENT AWAY FROM HOME, BUT HIS STAFF AT FORGE PARK DECLARE SUGGESTION OF ROBBERY ON DATE NAMED ENTIRELY UNFOUNDED. NAME OF BELL-EVART IS UNKNOWN TO THEM, THOUGH I HAVE ASCERTAINED THAT A MAJOR ALAN BELL-EVART, A BRITISHER, WAS GUEST AT A HOUSE IN NEIGHBOURHOOD ABOUT THAT TIME. NO CHARGE HAS EVER BEEN MADE AGAINST HIM, HOWEVER, AND UNDERSTAND HE PARTED FROM HIS HOST ON EXCELLENT TERMS. GLAD ASSIST FURTHER IN ANY WAY POSSIBLE.

Blake put down the cable, lighted his pipe.

First, the discovery that the dead man, Marius, was not, after all, a Scotland Yard man!

Now, the revelation that even the charge on which Raffles, alias Bell-Evart, had been "arrested" was a fake one!

Blake leaned back in his chair, his eyes narrowed, his pipe fuming. The entire case seemed to be going to pieces under his eyes, it did not make sense. If the "warrant" on which Raffles had been arrested was entirely implausible, the astute cracksman would have seen through it, and through "Detective-Inspector" Marius, in a second. Would he have allowed Marius to conduct him, as a prisoner, across half the world, from Melbourne to Gibraltar, if he had not genuinely believed Marius to be a Scotland Yard man? And if he had not believed Marius to be a detective, if he had not believed that he was to stand trial in England and that the trial was likely to go against him, would he have murdered Marius in the Bar Monte Cristo?

The answer to both questions was: "Improbable!"

Then try it, Blake thought, from another angle. Assume that Raffles had been duped by Marius, had believed him to be a Yard man. In that case, Marius' warrant must have carried conviction to the cracksman. Therefore, Raffles must have been mixed up in some way with a robbery, or attempted robbery, at Forge Park on the night of January 15th. And not merely an attempted robbery, of which the people of the house might have remained in ignorance, but a robbery "with violence". Yet Andrew Payne Hulburd and his staff denied knowledge of any such crime!

Was it possible that a robbery had, in fact, taken place —a robbery of which Raffles was guilty—that for some reason Andrew Payne Hulburd preferred to hush up? Blake had heard of such cases. For the sake of finding a working hypothesis, suppose this to be one of them. Now, Raffles was not a small-time crook. He went after the big prizes. If he had got away with something from Forge Park, it was something worth having. And if for private reasons, Andrew Payne Hulburd did not want police help in its recovery, what would the millionaire most likely do?

Try to recover it himself! Employ a man or men to trace and capture Raffles! But if they caught up with him in a remote place—say, Melbourne—and desired to bring him in person before Andrew Payne Hulburd, how were they, who had no official status, to take him as a prisoner across half the world? Obviously, by assuming official status!

Blake drew a long breath.

For the purposes of a working hypothesis, "Detective-Inspector" Marius was explained!

But the explanation—though it was a basis to work on —was still full of holes. Why an English "detective"? Why an English "warrant"? Why not have taken the "prisoner" directly from Melbourne to the United States? And how did it come about that "Detective-Inspector" Marius had been for years a patron of the Bar Monte Cristo, in Gibraltar?

When Captain Adam, pink-faced and bulky, in riding-breeches, light khaki drill tunic and sun-helmet, came striding in to fetch Blake for lunch, he found the criminologist fathoms deep in tobacco smoke and thought. He was ready for lunch, however, though he insisted upon "that place opposite the Hindu store—Chundra, Khitagara & Co.'s—in Main Street."

"The Universal," said Captain Adam. "As you please —but why, particularly?"

The reason was, that Blake was not entirely satisfied that Manders' and Westray's objective overnight in that alley had been, in fact, the Bar Monte Cristo. He wanted to observe Chundra's more closely—and now, as he set down his wineglass, at that table in the window of the Cafe Universal, he inquired casually:

"Know anything about these Gibraltar Hindus?"

"Not much," said the Army detective—"except that they're up to the neck in the contraband trade with Spain. We had an example of that only last night—a pretty serious one, too. A bunch of them brushed up against our sentries out near the burning-ghats, on the other side of the Rock. One Tommy was wounded; a Gibraltarian boatman, from Catalan Bay, was shot dead; two Hindus were taken prisoner, one of them so badly hurt he'll probably die. Their boat was taken, too—a fishing-smack that was laying off and on Catalan Bay with no lights."

Blake set down his knife and fork with a peculiar deliberation.

"Captain," he said, "that's peculiarly interesting. Their cargo was taken, too?"

"No. They hadn't got it aboard at the time. The Hindus who were taken admit they were smuggling, but they won't say where the cargo's hidden."

Blake said nothing for a moment. He was gazing intently across the crowded, sun-smitten channel of Main Street at the Hindu store opposite.

"Captain," he said slowly, "I'd like to see those two Hindus—and the wounded Tommy."

"Easy enough. The Tommy's in the military hospital, the wounded Hindu's in the prison hospital, and the other Hindu's in clink. Don't forget the Marius and Sacarello inquests, though."

"You can cover them for me," Blake said.

"Right. They'll be purely formal, anyway, and the funerals'll take place immediately afterwards. To be brutal, this is a hot climate." He added: "You have an idea of some kind, haven't you?"

"An idea," Blake said, with a slight smile—"and a little experiment I want to make."

He glanced again across the street—and at that moment a big, open Packard taxi went by, filled with white-clad tourists, obviously just ashore. A string of tourist-filled taxis and horse-coaches followed.

"A ship just came in, apparently," said Captain Adam. "The *Llandnno Chief* crowd's not being allowed ashore. The captain wants them all aboard so that he can sail the moment he gets permission."

"The *Rex*, senor," said the waiter, who had approached their table as Captain Adam spoke. "These people are from the *Rex*—the crack Italian liner, New York to Genoa. She was due yesterday morning, ten o'clock, but a dock strike in New York held up her sailing. She's only just arrived."

Blake nodded. Dabbing his lips thoughtfully with the napkin in his brown, bandaged hand, he looked at Captain Adam as the waiter withdrew.

"You heard that? The *Rex* was due yesterday morning —just an hour or so before the due arrival time of the *Llandnno Chief*!"

The Army sleuth stared.

"What of it?"

"I'm not sure," Blake said, "but——" He broke off, was silent for a moment—gazing across Main Street at the plate-glass windows and rug-hung doorway of Chundra, Khitagara & Co.'s—then abruptly stood up. "Excuse me. I must 'phone."

The telephone was at the back of the dim, cool cafe,

up two steps, in the passage where the cabaret artistes had their dressing-rooms. With the *Rex* just in, an influx of tourists imminent, the cabaret was hastily preparing to go on the floor. Scantily clad chorus girls, a gipsy flamenco singer, a Spanish eccentric dancer costumed as a bull-fighter—these, and others hurrying along the passage, glanced incuriously at the tall man in the double-breasted blue coat and white flannels as he went to the telephone.

Blake spoke quietly into the mouthpiece:

"Dock Police Office." He was through almost at once. "Blake, headquarters, speaking. Give me the officer who's examining passports of *Rex* passengers coming ashore. Thanks." He waited, listening to the chatter and bustle of the cabaret artistes, his eyes resting thoughtfully on the door of the men's dressing-room. A voice quacked in his ear, and he turned again to the mouthpiece.

"Passport officer? Good. You have your list by you of passengers who've just come ashore off the *Rex*? Right. Run your eye down it for the name Andrew Payne Hulburd!"

Silence. Blake waited tensely, his shoulders hunched over the telephone, the earpiece in his bandaged hand. Abruptly:

"No such name here, Mr. Blake," quacked the voice in his ear. Then added, as Blake was about to speak: "Espera, espera! Hold on!"

Blake held on. It was some moments before the voice came again:

"Are you there? A passenger came to the window just as we were speaking, Mr. Blake. He presented a U.S. passport in the name of Andrew Payne Hulburd. You want him? He's not gone ten yards yet."

"That's all right," Blake said. He could scarcely keep a thrill of jubilation from his voice. "Is he going on to Genoa in the *Rex*, or leaving her here?"

"Leaving her here, sir. He gives the Peak Hotel as the address he intends to stay at."

"Excellent," Blake said. "Describe him."

There was a low-voiced conference at the other end of

the wire, then the voice quacked again in Blake's ear:

"He's a tall man, Mr. Blake—over six feet—gaunt, a bit stooped, very sun-tanned, clean-shaven, high-arched nose, dark eyes, a mass of white hair. He's dressed in a white Palm Beach suit. He has a manservant with him called Spendrake."

"First rate," Blake said. "That's all I want, thanks. Thanks a lot."

He hung up, turned from the telephone. His eyes went straight to the door of the men's dressing-room, which stood ajar. He pushed it open, went in. The four men there stared at him. The one dressed as a bull-fighter said:

"Que quiere, senor?"

With his bandaged hand Blake turned back the lapel of his coat, showing a Gibraltar Police badge. He spoke in Spanish:

"I want one of you to do me the favour of lending me his make-up box, that's all!"

CHAPTER 13

A SIGNAL FROM LAL CHUNDRA

EXACTLY twenty-six hours had passed since the *Llandnno Chief* had dropped her anchor outside the boomed harbour of Gibraltar.

The arrival, now, of the crack Italian mail liner, *Rex*, had caused the streets of Gibraltar closely to duplicate the appearance they had worn the same hour the day before, following the *Llandnno Chief*'s arrival.

Again the blazing hot, narrow channel of Main Street was thronged with white-clad, camera-armed tourists—this time from the *Rex*, so that everywhere was heard the American accent instead of the Australian. Again, the white-canopied gharries clip-clopped, and the big touring-car taxis honked, up and down Main Street. Again the Moorish hawkers in dingy robes, turbans or tarbushes, and with bare, henna-stained heels, vociferated from the gutters. Again the scouts outside the Hindu tourist-traps importuned the thronging visitors and caught their arms, trying to urge them into the shops.

All was noise and confusion, and blinding sun-glare.

Inside the Hindu store of Chundra, Khitagara & Co., it was dim and cool—though by no means quiet. The Hindu salesmen, in their immaculate ducks, were working at pressure. The glass-topped counters, with their glittering display of pseudo-Indian jewellery and ornaments, were lined with customers. It was clearly a moment when the proprietor should have been present.

But he was not.

In that dim room over the shop—that room in which Raffles had spent so many hours—Nanda Lal Chundra, that slender and deceptively youthful-looking Hindu, sat on a pouffe before the window. The closed shutters barred him with lines of light and shade. He was leaning a little forward, in his favourite attitude, his long, dark hands, with the yellow half-moons in the nails, hanging lax between his knees. The tinge of yellow in the tight skin over his cheekbones was to-day more noticeable; so, too, was the web of fine lines about his dark, brilliant, un-usually wide-open eyes.

Before him stood a thin, swarthy man in a faded blue linen suit and rope-soled shoes. He would have looked more familiar to most Gibraltarians had he had on his arm a basket covered with a starched, white napkin, the corner turned back to show the fresh pink of crayfish.

"Exactly what did you tell them?" the Hindu demanded, in a curiously soft, spitting Spanish. "I warn you, Pepe, that I intend to know."

"I have answered you," the crayfish pedlar said desperately. "All that they got from me, I have reported to you. Por Dios, he had a knife, I tell you! He threatened me with it. The American held me helpless, locking my arms behind me, clamping a hand across my mouth. The bath-taps were running. No outcry could have been heard. The Englishman tore the shirt from my chest.

He brought the knife close—close! Senor, he swore to brand me; he swore to cut the skin from my chest. He meant it. These men were desperate—deadly! I talked. Who would not, por Dios? But what they got from me, that I have told you, every word!"

The Hindu did not move. His immobility was extra-ordinary. Only his brilliant eyes, looking up at his servant, seemed alive—brilliant and merciless.

"Consider again, Pepe, what it may mean if you have not told me all that they got from you." Strangely suave was his voice, belying the bright cruelty of his eyes. "The American girl was in that back room, below, when Mukerji threw the stiletto that killed Marius. I told him to assure himself that the American girl had passed through to one of the other display rooms. He thought she had. An instant after he threw the knife, he saw her. She was standing in a corner of the room, partially concealed by a leather-and-ivory screen which she had been examining. Mukerji seized her at once, dragged her into the next room.

"Unfortunate, Pepe, but plainly we could not let her go. She had witnessed the murder. We had to keep her here.

"But her friend, the young American, Westray, knew she had come here—was insistent on the point. We tried to make him believe he was mistaken. Useless, of course! He left unsatisfied. Sooner or later when she failed to appear, he was bound to go to the police—to bring them here. Therefore, you were set to follow him, to prevent that at all costs—even that of murder.

"He fell in immediately with Manders, whom we know—or, rather, I know—to be partner of Raffles. Before you realise what is happening—your first piece of bungling, Pepe—they are at the Dock Police Office. You contrived to overhear what passed. That they did not report the girl's disappearance is fortunate for you, Pepe!

"And your next piece of bungling? You lose them, in the gardens of the Peak Hotel, during the dance there. Where did they go? You have no idea! From a scrap of conversation overheard between them in the gardens, you believe that it was not to the police they went—that, in fact, they feared the police. But you are not sure of that—and you have lost them. What do you do, then? You locate Westray's room. You lay in wait to kill him— to ensure that, if he has not been to the police in that interim during which you lost sight of him, then he never will go!"

"Both fear the police," the Spaniard said suddenly. "I do not know where they went during that time. I am only sure it was not to the police. Later, perhaps, when he was sure that something serious had indeed happened to the girl, the American might have over-rode his reason for not calling in the police, and have gone to them. Therefore, I designed to kill him."

"You 'designed', you 'designed'," Lal Chundra said, with a flash of savage impatience—"but at the crisis, you bungle. You fall into their hands—Manders' and Westray's. You answer their questions. The damage is done now; I cannot repair it. But at least you shall tell me what they learned from you. I must know that, if I am to anticipate and block their moves."

"They demanded, first," said the Spaniard, "why I had attempted Westray's life."

"You answered?"

"Manders' knife was at my chest," said Pepe bitterly. "I answered. I told them I was hired to kill Westray."

The Hindu was intent, leaning a little forward on the pouffe. The confused din of Main Street entered the room—the cries of pedlars, the clatter of gharry-wheels, the blare of klaxons. The sun through the closed shutters tiger-striped the Hindu, sitting there, with light and shade.

"I told them I was hired to kill Westray," the Spaniard repeated. "Previously I had been fairly sure that they were averse to calling in the police. Now, something in their manner, their attitude, their behaviour, convinced me that I need never have attempted Westray's life— because, never, in any circumstances, would they approach the police. I felt this. Naturally, it coloured my replies. So—I admitted that I had been hired to kill Westray. I admitted—the knife threatened me; I was afraid—I admitted that you had hired me."

The Hindu did not move, but his breath escaped between his teeth with a low, vicious, hissing sound.

"They then asked about the girl?"

"Yes."

"And you admitted that she was here, in my hands?"

"No. I swear, senor—I denied all knowledge of the girl. They believed me."

"Pepe Domingo," said the Hindu, with a strange, suave ferocity, "make no mistake on this point. It is the vital one. You are quite certain that, even with the knife at your chest, you did not admit that the girl was here?"

"I swear it," the Spaniard said desperately. "They tried me far, they pressed me—but I clung to my story. I swore ignorance of the girl."

The Hindu was silent for a moment, in thought. Then: "They let you go?"

"They conferred," said Pepe Domingo. "I did not hear what was said. Finally, they told me to get out by the way I had come. Senor, that proves my point. They fear the police. But for that they would have turned me in. As they could not, what were they to do with me? Hold me prisoner, there in the hotel? Impossible! Kill me? But they could not get rid of my body. So—perforce, they let me go!"

The Hindu did not seem to be listening.

"Manders is a criminal—an associate of Raffles," he said softly. "That he would not go to the police—that is natural. But this American, the young Westray—why should he fear the police? It is plain that he loves this girl, Drusilla Brook. She vanishes. And Westray throws in his lot with Manders, rather than go to the police. That is well for us, but—I do not understand it. It is mysterious."

He raised his gleaming eyes to the Spaniard.

"It is well for us, I say. And I say it, Pepe Domingo, because, though you have disclaimed all knowledge of the girl, you betrayed everything when you admitted that it was I who hired you. They will know that my only possible motive for seeking Westray's death is the fact that he saw the girl enter this store. Therefore they will know that she is still here! If they do not go to the police, that is well. Any other move they may make," he said, with an iron smile, "I think I am competent to block!" He went on quickly: "Two other things I must know. First, does Manders know of Marius' death? Second, does he know that Marius was not a Scotland Yard man?"

The Spaniard said uneasily:

"I let that slip. It was one word, spoken under stress, with that knife at my chest, that gave them a hint. They forced the rest from me. But I swear I did not tell them he was killed from this store. I withheld that. They think Raffles killed him."

Lal Chundra did not move.

"You have bungled intolerably, Pepe. You shall pay for it. You shall pay very heavily for it."

He clapped his slender hands, the door masked by the prayer-rug opened, a thick-set Hindu, with a small-pox pitted face entered softly.

"Go with Mukerji," said Lal Chundra.

Without a word the crayfish-pedlar left the room with the pockmarked Hindu.

Lal Chundra sat for some minutes motionless on the pouffe, leaning forward, his hands hanging lax between his knees. It was singular, the impression of youthfulness he gave, with his slight figure in its spotless white ducks, his thick, jet-black hair, his large, brilliant, jet-black eyes, his seemingly—at a distance—lineless face.

Finally he rose, passed out through the door covered by the prayer-rug.

Everywhere about this house was a faint scent of musk. It hung in the dark gloom of the narrow stairs down which he passed. It was in the brilliant sunlight which flooded the showroom into which the stairs opened.

Set about with glass-topped showcases, hung with pseudo-Moorish leatherwork and Spanish shawls, this sun-bright, musk-scented room was the one which faced the Bar Monte Cristo across the alley.

The room was empty.

Automatically as he crossed it, Lal Chundra glanced through the big, open window at the corresponding window of the Bar Monte Cristo, opposite.

He stopped dead.

Sitting before the open window in the Bar Monte Cristo was a man in white ducks and panama. He held a handkerchief to his face, as though to shield it; but the slant of the panama, the set of the shoulders, the man's attitude in the chair, betrayed him instantly to the Hindu as Raffles!

The man opposite raised his right hand, pointing across the alley. The gesture was unmistakable. Should he come across?

The Hindu's mind worked swiftly. The escape attempt last night had failed. One of his men was in prison, another in the prison hospital, and the third had escaped and got back. He had reported that Raffles, too, had escaped, but was lost. Now, here he was! He had got rid of the Hindu disguise. He was back here seeking shelter, but had had the sense not to walk straight in. His gesture was plain: Was the coast clear? Could he come across?

The Hindu, staring across the alley, shook his head—slowly, warningly, emphatically. His lips, moving soundlessly, exaggerating the outline of the words, signalled:

"After dark! After dark!"

In the window of that dim room across the sun-glaring alley, the man with the handkerchief to his face nodded his head.

Lal Chundra turned and, passing through the bead curtain, walked rapidly into his shop.

He returned to the back room five minutes later. He was aghast at Raffles' daring in returning thus to the scene of Marius' murder. Yet, Lal Chundra thought, there was this angle—the Bar Monte Cristo was the last place in which the police would seek "Bell-Evart". Provided he had been able to pass the waiter unrecognised, the Bar Monte Cristo might be for Raffles, for a few hours, a safe hide-out.

Returning to the back room Lal Chundra glanced across again at the window opposite. Someone had closed the shutters.

The Hindu nodded thoughtfully. Yes, Raffles was clever. He knew what he was about. Killing time in that dim room of the Bar Monte Cristo, behind those closed shutters—reading, occasionally ordering a drink, keeping his face hidden—Raffles should be safe, with luck, until after dark! Then a new method must be contrived, a new attempt made, to get the cracksman out of Gibraltar. For until he was out of it, safe, he—Lal Chundra—could not hope to get his hands on the Weyman manuscript!

The Hindu went back through the bead curtain into his shop, thinking deeply.

He might have thought still more deeply—or, on the other hand, his thought processes might have been completely paralysed—had he dreamed that, through a section of slat carefully removed from the shutters, he was watched by the grey, deep-set eyes of the adroit Mr. Blake, in that room in the Bar Monte Cristo!

When Lal Chundra went back through the bead curtain into his shop, Blake turned from the shuttered window opposite.

He was alone in the dim, cool room. He took off his panama, tossed it on to one of the low, Moorish tables, and, feeling for pipe and pouch, dropped into a cane chair.

He was exceedingly pleased with the result of his little experiment. It had been a long shot, but it had come off.

Captain Kerry Adam's mention of a brush between Hindu contraband-runners and British sentries had given him the idea. Why, he had wondered, had the contraband-runners' cargo not been found? A possible answer was, that that cargo was capable of volition on its own account—of running away on its own legs; in other words that the cargo those Hindus had been trying to smuggle out of Gib was a man! Assuming this possibility, what man was more desperately anxious to get off the Rock than A. J. Raffles, alias Major Alan Bell-Evart?

The idea was suggestive, but it meant that Raffles must be acquainted with, and be receiving the assistance of, Gibraltar Hindus. If this were so, then Manders' and Westray's presence in Chundra's backyard last night was to a certain extent explained. Their presence there had something to do with Raffles, who, in turn, must have something to do with Chundra's.

But this was all theoretical. How was he to test it?

If Raffles had been with those Hindus last night, and if —which was not proved—those Hindus were from Chundra's store, then the probability was that it was the store which had been his place of shelter. With the failure of the attempt to escape in the fishing-smack, Raffles, though not captured, must be still on the Rock. Was it not likely that he would return to the people who were helping him, giving him shelter?

Suddenly, Blake's idea flashed upon him. If he could contrive to make the people in Chundra's think he was Raffles—if he could signal them, and get a reply to his signal—there would be certain proof that it was from Chundra's store that Raffles was receiving help. How was the experiment to be worked, though? He could not hope to pass as Raffles except at a distance. Suddenly he remembered that window in the Bar Monte Cristo which faced the window in Chundra's. The rest was easy. From the "Bell-Evart" radio descriptions, he knew Raffles had worn a white duck suit and a panama. A touch of make-up about the eyes and eyebrows. Keep his face covered as much as possible, as a man would whom the police were after——

The experiment had been a complete success. That youthful-looking Hindu—was he the boss?—had answered the signal of the man he believed to be Raffles, and thereby had betrayed himself. "After dark", he had mouthed, to be lip-read; "After dark!"

Now, as Blake thoughtfully filled his pipe, behind the closed shutters in that dim room in the Bar Monte Cristo, he considered the implications of his discovery.

Out of the unholy tangle, now, there were beginning to emerge leading strings. He seized upon them, classified them. Thus:

1. Raffles was not a killer. That was a psychological fact. If Raffles had run true to character, he had not killed the pseudo-detective, Marius. Therefore, it was a hundred to one that he had not killed Inspector Sacarello.

2. Chundra, Khitagara & Co., it was now proven, were implicated with Raffles. Marius had died in this room. Raffles, Blake felt sure, had not killed him; but because Raffles was so placed that |circumstantial evidence indicated his guilt, the cracksman had bolted.

3. From the first, Inspector Sacarello's murder had seemed to Blake to imply the hand of a Gibraltarian, since the murderer must have known of Sacarello's friendship with Captain Adam, and his habit of consulting the Intelligence man.

4. Marius had died from a stiletto in the back—"a stiletto", to quote Dr. Azzopardi's description of that vanished weapon, "with an ivory hilt carven into the likeness of an elephant's head and trunk". Who, in Gibraltar, dealt in just such articles as ivory-hilted stilettos? Answer—Hindus!

5. A stiletto can be thrown as well as thrust. The window of this room in which Marius had died squarely faced a window in Chundra's store. Suppose the stiletto to have been thrown from that window, then Raffles would have found himself alone in this room with a dead man— motive and opportunity provable against him. No wonder Raffles had bolted!

Smoking hard, Blake nodded to himself.

"That was what happened. It must have happened like that."

He continued with his classifications:

6. Marius had been killed by a person, or by persons, in Chundra's store. Subsequently that same concern had sheltered Raffles, had tried to smuggle him out of Gibraltar. For this there could be only one sane explanation. The Hindus had killed Marius in order to place Raffles in a murder jam—and thus, if they could make him believe that they alone could extricate him from it, in their power. For what purpose? The answer was glaring —bargaining! The Hindus wanted something from Raffles. In return for it, they offered him a way out from the murder jam—a way of escape from the Rock.

7. There was the motive of Sacarello's murder. Blake knew that "Bell-Evart" was in reality Raffles. But he could not prove it. With all exhibits in the Marius murder destroyed, it could never be proved that "Bell-Evart" was in reality Raffles. Therefore, the destruction of those exhibits must have been part of the Hindus' bargain with Raffles. Therefore, the Hindus had killed Sacarello.

8. What did the Hindus want from Raffles in return for all this? Almost certainly what they wanted was the object which Raffles—if Blake were correct in his earlier deduction that a robbery had taken place at Forge Park in January which the victims were hushing up—had stolen from the Andrew Payne Hulburd estate.

At this stage in his reflections, Blake lighted his third pipe. He had come far. His theory untied a good many knots. It held together. It was comprehensible. But there were still certain knots that defied him. They were these:

1. Who was this Dan Westray—this young American who, as Blake had learned aboard the *Llandnno Chief*, had joined the ship at Port Said, had done his utmost to monopolise his countrywoman, the girl Drusilla Brook, and subsequently, inexplicably, had thrown in his lot with Raffles' partner, Bunny Manders?

2. Who was Drusilla Brook—this by all accounts lovely creature who, likewise joining the ship at Port Said, had displayed an acute interest in "Major Bell-Evart", and then, arriving here in Gibraltar, had seemingly vanished?

3. If Blake were right in his earlier deduction that the pseudo-detective Marius was actually an agent employed by Andrew Payne Hulburd to recover, privately, that which had been stolen from Forge Park, how did it come about that for years, on and off, Marius had been a visitor to Gibraltar? There was something strange about that.

The idea which had led Blake to 'phone the Dock Police Office to ask if Andrew Payne Hulburd had come in on the *Rex* had been simply enough arrived at. Assuming Marius to be the millionaire's agent; assuming him to have cabled Hulburd, from some port along the *Llandnno Chief*'s route, that he held the Forge Park robber captive; assuming Hulburd to be anxious to recover quickly that which had been stolen—what, then, more likely than that Hulburd should catch the *Rex* with a view to meeting his agent and the prisoner en route? The *Rex* had been due at Gibraltar yesterday, from New York, some hours before the expected arrival time of the *Llandnno Chief*, from the East.

A neat deduction on Blake's part—and, as his 'phone call to the Dock Police Office proved, a correct one. Andrew Payne Hulburd was in Gibraltar. But it still seemed strange to Blake that Marius, Hulburd's agent, presumably hired in America, should be a man known by appearance, over a course of years, right here at the Bar Monte Cristo.

Blake was smoking his fourth pipe over these still unravelled knots when the bead curtain behind him was suddenly swept aside, and Tinker entered.

"Guv'nor"—the young man was flushed, breathing quickly—"jingo, I've been hunting all over town for you!"

"What's wrong?"

"I've lost 'em!"

"Manders and Westray?" Blake was instantly alert, sitting up in the cane chair, knocking out his pipe. "What happened?"

"They put one over on me," Tinker said bitterly. "Gosh, I'm sorry, guv'! They left the Peak Hotel just before two. They took a gharry, drove to the Theatre Royal, off Main Street. It's a cinema. There's a matinee today. They took tickets and went in. Or I thought they went in. I was close after 'em, but when I got inside, although the show hadn't started and the lights were on, there wasn't a sign of 'em. I reckon they ducked into a room off the stairs on the way up to the circle—and I went blinding by and missed 'em. They must have been wise to me, guv', though I'd have sworn they had no idea I was tailing 'em."

Blake said dryly:

"They may merely have been taking safeguards on general principles. They've gone to rendezvous somewhere with Raffles, of course. Well, the damage is done. Don't worry, old son. Get back to their hotel—wait for 'em; and, incidentally, keep your eye on a new guest who's just arrived there. Mr. Andrew Payne Hulburd, the American millionaire."

"Right, guv'nor. Will you be here if I want to get in touch with you?"

"No," Blake said. "Try headquarters if you need me. I'm just going up to the prison—and the prison hospital."

Tinker left, by the side entrance. Blake clapped his hands for Jose—that soft-footed waiter who, since his attempt to pick Marius' pocket and his consequent shocking discovery that the man was dead, had known precious little peace of mind.

Blake sent Jose for a bowl of water and a towel. He cleaned off the few skilful touches of make-up about his eyes and eyebrows. Lack of material in that borrowed make-up box had prevented his trying to reproduce Raffles' neat, close-clipped moustache—which was one reason why he had kept that handkerchief to his face. (Blake had been lucky here, though he didn't know it. Had he reproduced Raffles' moustache, he would never have deceived Lal Chundra—for the Hindu had seen Raffles shave his moustache, the night before!)

As Blake had told Tinker, it was his intention to visit

the gaoled Hindu, the Hindu in the prison hospital, and also the wounded Tommy.

But, after leaving the Bar Monte Cristo—by the side entrance, down the alley, out of eyeshot of Chundra's—Blake went first to police headquarters.

Captain Adam, who had promised to report to Blake there on the Marius and Sacarello inquests, had not yet arrived. Likewise, because of the inquests, headquarters was unusually free of newspapermen, who were reaping a harvest of headlines from this Gibraltar business, and were keeping the cables humming.

Inspector Parodi and Sergeant Mifsud were waiting for Blake, and the mountainous sergeant had the first word:

"Mr. Blake, it is certain now—she has disappeared!"

"The American girl?"

"Si! Drusilla Brook! Already, the radio station has twice broadcast her name and description, with a request as to her whereabouts. They will continue to repeat the call—but if she is just staying, in a normal way, with some private resident, it is certain we should have heard by now. Everybody on the Rock, you may be sure, has heard those calls or heard of them. Yet—we have received no information. It is certain, now, either that she is in hiding, or——"

"Or?" Blake said grimly.

"Or something has happened to her," said Sergeant Mifsud.

Blake filled his pipe thoughtfully.

"Keep those radio calls going out, sergeant. The deeper I go in this case, the more certain I am that that girl is the key to our mystery. Meantime"—he turned to Inspector Parodi—"I want some plainclothes men—four or five of them. You know the Hindu store—Chundra, Khitagara's—on Main Street?"

"Chundra's? Yes."

"I want them posted to watch that store. Two men in the Bar Monte Cristo, to keep an eye on that side window of Chundra's. One man in the Cafe Universal, on Main

Street, opposite the front entrance. If there are any other entrances or exits, I want them covered. They're to watch for anybody who looks remotely like 'Major Alan Bell-Evart'. If they see any such person enter, they're to telephone headquarters here instantly. They must be good men, inspector. Nobody in that store must know that the place is watched."

"I have the men," said the young inspector.

"Good," Blake said. "I don't think we're far off an arrest now—quite a number of arrests, in fact!"

Thirty-five minutes later, he was again speaking to Inspector Parodi—this time over the telephone from the Military Hospital:

"You have your men placed round Chundra's?"

"Yes."

"Can you get a message to each of them—quickly and quietly?"

"Yes, sir."

"Tell them this." Blake's voice came crisply over the wire. "They've all heard the 'Bell-Evart' radio descriptions. They know the height and build of the man they're after. In addition to this—he's disguised as a Hindu and is wearing tinted glasses!"

CHAPTER 14

STAFF WORK

DISGUISED as a Hindu and wearing tinted glasses, but fatally unaware that his description was now known to Blake—unaware, even, that his arch-enemy was directing the pursuit—Raffles sat at a table at the far end of that tunnel in the casemate wall which was called the Cafe Obrero.

He had been there for nearly two hours. His anxiety was acute. He lighted one cigarette from the stub of another, in an endless chain, his lean fingers, stained to coffee colour by the make-up given him by Lal Chundra, endlessly kneaded bread-pills on his plate; his eyes, behind the tinted glasses, rarely left that square of sunshine which was the entrance to the cafe in the casemates.

No sign of Bunny!

With the passing of every minute, Raffles' suspense increased. There were so many things, so many disasters, which might have happened. His brain was fertile in picturing them. The chief, and grisliest, of them was that the police might have discovered Bunny's connection with him, and foreseeing the possibility of his getting in touch with Bunny, have tapped the Peak Hotel telephone wire.

It was that fear which had caused him to disguise his voice, and make his message appear innocuous, when he had telephoned his partner. Bunny was quick. He'd grasp the significance of the message. But suppose the police, too, had grasped its significance? Then they'd hold Bunny, for one thing. For another, they'd send men to the Cafe Obrero. If police came walking in now, through that square of sunshine at the end of the tunnel there, the jig was up. He had no weapon. He wouldn't have a cat's chance. Not a——

He sat stockstill. From the flat glare of the sun outside, two men in white ducks had walked into the hot, odorous gloom of the casemate cafe.

Bunny Manders and—Raffles didn't know how to take this—Dan Westray, Jun., the American!

What the devil was Bunny doing here in company with Dan Westray? Raffles sat taut—wary, suspicious, acutely watchful.

The two men stood just inside the entrance, in that involuntary pause imposed by the gloom within after the blinding glare outside.

Raffles risked it. After all, Bunny would never have brought Westray here unless he were sure of him. Raffles struck his hands together, called:

"Hola, amigos!"

Bunny saw the "Hindu" then, and walked down

between the tables towards him, Westray following. The two sat down at Raffles' table, Bunny murmuring:

"Westray's with us! He knows how things stand!"

The lanky young American grinned.

"I'd know you, Bell-Evart"—he kept his voice low—"or, rather, Raffles—oh yes, Bunny's come clean—even though you seem to have caught the sun since I saw you, last! Don't worry. I'm in with you, as Manders says—ear-deep! Manders'll explain——"

Raffles clapped his hands for the waiter-proprietor, ordered wine in his babu English. When the padrone had withdrawn, Raffles looked keenly at Bunny through his tinted glasses. This was the first meeting of the partners for many months, but there was no time for anything but straight-to-the-point talk. And with nobody at the nearby tables, they could talk with safety. Raffles said at once:

"Bunny, old scout, there's one thing I must know straight away. A deuce of a lot depends on it. Did you bring my passport from England?"

Bunny put a hand in the pocket of his pin-stripe, double-breasted grey coat, drew out Raffles' passport—his real one, the one in his own name.

The cracksman took it with a deep sigh of relief.

"Man, that's taken ten years off me!" He pocketed the passport. "Right! Now, then—let's hear how things stand with you."

Bunny swiftly explained what had happened to him, how he had fallen in with Dan Westray, how they had visited Chundra's overnight, how they had encountered—of all people—Blake the criminologist.

"Blake!" Raffles exclaimed. "Blake! Blake here in Gib?"

"Not merely that," Bunny said, "but he's on the case. He's after you!"

The curious, tense deliberation with which Raffles took a cigarette from his box, the care with which he lighted it, the hard tightening of his mouth—all betrayed the shock which the news was to him. But his voice was calm—hard and calm:

"Go on."

Bunny told Raffles how that morning he had caught a glimpse in the lobby of the Peak Hotel, of Blake's assistant, Tinker.

"Naturally, when your 'phone call came, we took precautions before answering it. Tinker followed us when we left the hotel—but we shook him, all right."

Raffles' eyes flickered to the square of hard sunlight which was the cafe entrance.

"I hope you're sure of that!"

"We shouldn't have come here," said Bunny, "if we hadn't been sure." He went on to tell of the crayfish pedlar's attempt on Dan Westray's life. "A. J., what was the charge you were pinched on, in Melbourne?"

"Robbery," Raffles said, "robbery with violence at Forge Park, Westchester County, on the night of January 15th."

Dan Westray leaned forward quickly to put his foot on the cigarette he had just dropped on the concrete floor. But he was not so quick that Raffles missed the sudden gleam in his eyes.

"It's a cooked-up charge," Bunny said. "I've got some good news for you, A.J.! We got it from the crayfish pedlar. You may or may not know it, but Marius was an imposter. He was no more a Yard man than I am!"

Raffles leaned back in his chair, staring. This news was even more of a shock to him than that of Blake's presence in Gib. He had never doubted Marius' bona fides. He had wondered, true, why he should have been arrested on an English, not an American, warrant. But he had come half-across the world with Marius, as a prisoner, and never doubted the man's position. He felt again that tap on his shoulder—that tap which had been like the crack of doom—as he sat in shirtsleeves in the stand on Melbourne Cricket Ground watching Stan McCabe's crisp, powerful hooking. He saw again Marius' weather-red face, long upper lip, read again the word on the warrant for "Major Bell-Evart", heard Marius' hard, quiet voice: "Sorry, major—get your coat on and get moving!" By God, he had been taken in all along the line! Or had he? It was hard to believe.

"Bunny—man alive, let me get this straight! Are you sure—one hundred per cent certain——"

"Listen," Bunny said, and talked. And when he had finished:

"Well—there's not much doubt about it," Raffles said. "And I gave that fake dick my parole not to attempt escape if we went ashore." He was silent for a moment then: "But get this! I was taken in by Marius' warrant, but I had good reason to be. There was a robbery at Forge Park on the night of January 15th, and I know it. I was there. I was there with intent to rob Andrew Payne Hulburd's safe. But I didn't do it. Somebody beat me to it, and they got away with an object called the Weyman Manuscript. Lal Chundra wants that manuscript, and he thinks I've got it—that I've parked it somewhere in safe deposit under a false name.

"Wait! Why, the truth sticks out now like a sore thumb! Marius knew Gib like a book; Marius knew all about Chundra's. Sure! And why? Marius was Chundra's man! Chundra knew all about that Weyman Manuscript. He wanted it—I don't know why, I don't even know what the Weyman Manuscript is! Marius was one of the cracksmen whom Chundra himself told me he employed. Marius was sent to steal the Weyman Manuscript from Forge Park. But someone beat him to it. He thought it was me. He thought I had the manuscript. He traced me, caught up with me in Melbourne, posed as a Yard man so as to be able to bring me to Gib.

"He took me to the Bar Monte Cristo. Why? Because it has a window facing Chundra's; because his instructions were to take me there and watch for the O.K. signal from Chundra to take me across to the store. Of course, of course!"

Raffles' eyes gleamed blue behind the tinted glasses. He was like a man talking to himself, in a cold fever of penetration.

"That's why he was bragging to me about the 'power'

of Chundra's, its 'secret business'—he was bragging about his own organisation, the organisation that employed him. He thought it safe to brag; he had me where he wanted me.

"But Chundra didn't give him the O.K. signal. No! That crafty, cold-blooded Hindu knew a trick worth two of that. He wanted me utterly in his power, he wanted a hold on me—a bargaining hold. So he had his own man, Marius, killed—to put me in a murder jam, from which he would offer to extricate me in exchange for my turning over to him the Weyman Manuscript! All plain sailing. He thought the game was in the bag, but there was a slip somewhere—the American girl, Drusilla Brook, witnessed the murder of Marius. So he was forced to hold her—to——"

He broke off, glancing at Westray. The young American was white under his tan; there was sweat on his forehead.

"Finish it, Raffles," he said, with an icy harshness.

"To silence her—— She's a murder witness. If you're right, she knows enough to hang Chundra. To hold her temporarily—silence her temporarily—what good would that be? She's either dead, or she soon will be!"

Westray drove a clenched fist into the open palm of his other hand. His blue eyes were tortured.

"I blame myself. I should have gone to the police earlier. I had a reason for not going—a strong one, a private one. But it's nothing—nothing, I tell you—compared with the life or death of that girl. I'm going to the police right now!"

Raffles' dark-stained hand shot out, closing on the young American's wrist.

"Wait! Listen to me! If you go to the police now, Westray, you'll blow Bunny and me sky-high—sky-high! They know you've been running around with Bunny. Blake knows Bunny is my partner. If you go to the police, you'll see Blake. He's one of the cleverest dicks alive. He'll grill you. He'll break you down with his questions. He'll get the whole yarn out of you. It may or may not save the girl, but it'll certainly be the finish for Bunny and me!

"I've a better plan—better for Drusilla, better for us. Risky—I admit that. But the risk'll be mainly mine.

"Listen now! Chundra knows by now what happened last night at the burning-ghats. He knows I'm still at large. The bargain between us stands—that he gets me out of Gib in exchange for my handing to his agents the Weyman Manuscript, which he thinks I've hidden somewhere. Now, if I return to Chundra's he'll let me in. He'll think I've returned to him for shelter, for a new attempt to be made to get me off the Rock.

"Once in, I'll undertake to find out what's happened to Drusilla. He may have moved her from the store. He may have killed her. If she lives, Westray, I'll get her out—with you two in that backyard to help.

"It's as vital to me that Drusilla should be saved, if she's alive, as it is to you. One charge against me is scotched already—Marius' warrant, on the Forge Park Case, was fake. That lets me out. But I'm wanted for Marius' murder—of which, it's now plain, Drusilla was a witness—of which she can clear me!"

Bunny said quickly:

"If you go back to that store, and fail——"

"That's my bad luck," said Raffles. "I'm taking the chance. I'm going to stay put in this cafe until well after dark, and then——" He broke off. "Have you got a gun, Bunny?"

"I've an automatic on me. I've another in my case at the hotel."

"I'll have the one that's on you," said Raffles.

He struck his hands together. The fat padron waddled down between the tables. With a flash of white teeth in his dusky, dark-spectacled countenance, "Rabaji Ram Dass" ordered wine.

The entrance of the cafe in the casemates still framed a square of brilliant sunshine; at the tables near the entrance the cocheros and taxi-drivers quarrelled over their cards;

flies buzzed in the hot gloom about the hams and salamis pendant from the ceiling.

The wine came. Raffles filled their three glasses.

"It's sink or swim tonight," he said. "If we can rescue Drusilla, she'll have something to be grateful for—and so shall I! If she clears me of Marius' murder, the only thing left for Blake to charge me on is forging a passport. He could get me seven years on that—but to do it, he's got to prove that 'Bell-Evart' and Raffles are the same man. And to do that, he's got to catch me right here on this Rock—and I'm not caught yet! Salud, amigos!"

They drank.

"Now," said Raffles, as he put down his glass; "now for a little staff-work——"

The three partners were careful about that staff-work. As far as possible, they made allowances for every contingency. They were undertaking a dangerous gamble, and knew it. The chief threat was that, after his encounter with Bunny and Dan last night in Chundra's yard, Blake might have set a man to watch the store.

"If so, he's your pigeon," Raffles said. "Any stray party lurking round that store it's your business to jump! And he hasn't got to see who jumps him, either! Understand?"

They understood.

What they did not know—when they left Raffles there in the casemate cafe and headed back for the Peak Hotel—was that Blake had posted, not one man to watch Chundra's, but a cordon of five! What they did not know, either, was that Blake was aware of Raffles' disguise as a Hindu with tinted glasses!

Raffles' staff-work might be good.

But Blake's was better!

.   .   .   .   .

Blake, at the time he 'phoned Inspector Parodi and told him of the disguise Raffles had adopted, was at the Military Hospital.

Ten minutes at the bedside of the sentry wounded in

the brush with Hindus out near the burning-ghats had proved highly illuminating. The interview had corroborated the accuracy of Blake's idea that the "cargo" which those Hindus had been smuggling off the Rock was a living one—a man—Raffles!

Cockneys are tough. Cockneys in khaki are pretty well indestructible. This one sat up in bed, with his left arm and shoulder swathed in bandages, and scoffed the grapes brought him by the tactful Mr. Blake.

"I 'ears a bit of a noise, sir—like it might be footsteps in the sand," said the Cockney. "I creeps up close—an' sees figures cuttin' across the beach from the wall of the burnin'-ghats. That's enough for me. I comes out wiv a challenge: "Altoogozeair!" No answer. I creeps closer. I bin on duty some time, an' me eyes is used to the dark, so I can almost see in it, like a blinkin' cat—you know how you can sometimes. I didn't think they could see me, bein' as I got the wall be'ind me—but I could see them, all right: five of 'em! I'm just about to challenge again when one of 'em outs wiv a knife. Crikey, if he'd chucked it, he'd 'a' had me skewered like a whelk. Talk about cat's eyes! That bloke saw me, all right! But before 'e could chuck his knife, the bloke next 'im lets fly a pippin of a left hook an' lays the bloke with the knife colder'n an eel!"

Blake drew a deep breath. He was smiling, pipe clamped between his teeth. "Ever heard of a Hindu with a left hook before, Nobby?"

"No, dog bite me," said Nobby, "I ain't! But this'n was a Hindu all right. When 'e 'it 'is mate, I brings my rifle up and let 'em have it—and the second I fires, on flashes the searchlight up on the Rock. I see 'em all then, for an instant, lit up like the Palladium stage—an' this codger with the left hook is a Hindu, an' he's got dark glasses on!"

"And then," said Blake, "one of them shot you—but it wasn't the one with the dark glasses, Nobby!"

Nobby stared. "You're right, sir—nor it weren't. But 'ow the— 'scuse me—'ow did you know?"

Blake took his pipe from his mouth, looked thoughtfully at the stem, from which a wisp of smoke curled.

"As you know, Nobby, I'm a detective. I'm after a certain man. That man is one of the cleverest cracksmen alive. He's also one of the best sportsmen I ever met. He saved your life last night, Nobby—and it'll probably cost him his liberty!"

Blake stood up.

"Fond of cricket?"

"Yessir."

"Then you know his name as well as I do," Blake said. "Good-bye, Nobby—don't give yourself appendicitis with those grapes!"

Blake went out. Left alone, Nobby stared unseeingly out of the window at the wide, blue sweep of the bay, with the white ship, the *Llandnno Chief*, lying at anchor, and the red hills of Spain far in the distance.

"Famous cricketer," Nobby muttered. "Know 'is name well——"

Downstairs, Blake was telephoning to Inspector Parodi his description of A. J. Raffles' disguise as a Hindu with tinted spectacles.

.   .   .   .   .

Blake's assistant was equally busy. You would not have thought it, however, to look at him.

Tinker reclined practically upon his shoulder-blades in a chromium easy-chair in the lounge of the Peak Hotel. It was a spacious lounge, its vast area of black-and-white tiled floor dotted with low tables set about with chromium chairs. Round most of the tables were little tea-party groups of khaki-uniformed Army officers, white-uniformed Navy officers, and summery-frocked ladies of the garrison. A gay buzz of chatter competed with the blaring music of a loudspeaker.

Here and there about the lounge stood disc gambling-machines, and big glass-and-chromium showcases containing near-cloisonne, fake brasswork, Moroccingham leather, and such other "souvenirs" as tourists lust after.

Tinker's chair was tucked away in a corner behind one of these showcases. Through the glass of the showcase, Tinker's alert eyes were fixed upon the leonine white head of a tall man who sat just the other side of the showcase, with his back to it. The man was the American millionaire and philanthropical godfather of scientists and inventors, Andrew Payne Hulburd, of Forge Park.

"Keep an eye on him," Blake had said—and Tinker was doing so.

He had already made a discovery of acute interest. Returning to the hotel from his talk with Blake, Tinker's first act had been to assure himself that Andrew Payne Hulburd had registered. The elegant young Swiss in charge of the reception desk, to whom Tinker had earlier that day made known the fact that he was working for the police, had shown him Hulburd's signature in the register. The Swiss added:

"He's up in his room, now—three-o-two. His valet, Spendrake, is on the floor above—four-seven-five. By the way, when Mr. Hulburd registered he happened to see this name—just above his own. He asked if the gentleman was in, and if not, when he would be back. He seemed sort of anxious to know, but I wasn't able to tell him."

The signature to which the Swiss's manicured finger had pointed was that of Dan Westray, Jun.!

The millionaire had come downstairs shortly afterwards —a tall, gaunt man, of striking appearance, with his darkly tanned face, dark eyes, and leonine, white head. He had chosen a cane settee in a corner of the lounge—a corner, Tinker noticed, from which the swinging glass doors could be seen—and ordered a John Collins.

Tinker had taken up a position behind the showcase, through which, unobserved, he could watch both Hulburd and the doors. He had been here, now, for some time, the American was on his third John Collins and his second cigar, and Tinker was beginning to chafe at the inaction, when the hall-porter swung the doors open and Bunny Manders walked in with the long-legged young American, Westray.

Tinker wedged his shoulders lower in the chromium chair, held an open *Tatler* before his face. But his eyes watched keenly through the miscellany of articles in the big showcase.

Hulburd beckoned a waiter.

"Ask that gentleman"—the American was so close that his voice was clearly audible to Tinker—"the tall one, just going over toward the stairs, if he'll step across here for a moment."

The waiter nodded, threaded his way quickly between the tables, caught up with Manders and Westray as they reached the foot of the stairs. He spoke to Westray. Both men turned and looked across the lounge. Manders had a spare eyeglass, Tinker noticed! That Westray was startled, his expression showed. He turned and spoke to Bunny Manders, who nodded and went on up the stairs.

Dan Westray threaded his way between the tables.

Tinker kept perfectly still behind the showcase, holding the *Tatler* before his face. He heard Westray's voice clearly:

"Gosh, sir! This is a surprise! You here!"

They shook hands.

"Sit down, Dan," said the millionaire. "I got your cable from Aden, saying you'd be joining the *Llandnno Chief* at Port Said—and why you'd be joining her. In the circumstances, I thought it as well to come over. I thought, if I jumped the *Rex*, I'd get here just in time to intercept you—should have done, too, but the *Rex* lost a day through a dock strike. As it is, I'm lucky to find you still here. I didn't radio you on the *Llandnno Chief* —didn't want anybody to get wise to the fact that you're my stepson. Nobody here knows, I guess?"

"Not a soul, sir."

"Well, what's happening, Dan? You did a fine job to locate her at all, but—how do you stand now? You've established some sort of contact?"

"I——" Dan broke off. "Listen, sir!"

In a brief lull in the music from the loudspeaker, the voice of the announcer was blaring:

"——from the *Llandnno Chief*, on which she is a passenger. No response having been received by Inspector Parodi to earlier broadcasts this afternoon, it is feared Miss Brook may have met with some mishap. Here is her description: Height, five feet, eight inches; of slender build; complexion, golden-brown; very fair, almost flaxen hair; grey eyes. Is wearing a white frock, it is believed, and small white hat. Any information to Inspector Parodi."

Through the glass of the showcase, Tinker could see Dan Westray's face in profile—young, good-looking, but at the moment very grim.

"There's your answer, sir!"

"But, Dan"—the millionaire's voice was so low that Tinker could scarcely hear it—" 'missing'! What does this mean?"

Westray glanced about him.

"Better come upstairs, sir."

Tinker cursed as the two Americans moved away across the crowded, noisy lounge. The moment they had passed from view up the wide, curving staircase, he emerged from his hiding-place and made a dive for the nearest 'phone.

. . . . .

Blake had just returned to police headquarters after visiting the wounded Nobby, the Hindu in prison, and the Hindu in the prison hospital. The latter, he had learned, had died an hour before. His identity had not yet been established. The other Hindu—who bore the evidences, in the form of a bruised mouth and a shortage of front teeth, of the left hook which had put him to sleep —likewise was sullenly withholding his name, and the name of the man for whom he had been working.

Blake had got nothing from the interview. But he had not been two minutes back at police headquarters when the telephone on the late Inspector Sacarello's desk rang urgently, and, taking up the receiver, he heard Tinker's voice.

Blake listened. He asked no questions, but a glitter came into his grey, deep-set eyes as he listened. He said finally:

"Stay with it, Tinker!"

He hooked up, sat for a full minute motionless in deep thought. Suddenly he rose, went out with long strides to the charge-room. Inspector Parodi was there. Blake said urgently:

"Inspector, has the *Llandnno Chief* cleared yet?"

"You said you'd finished with her, Mr. Blake. I gave her her clearance papers half-an-hour ago!"

Blake snapped his fingers.

"We've got to catch that ship! Get on that 'phone to the dock police, inspector—and the radio station if necessary. If the *Llandnno Chief* has left, she must put back! She must be stopped at all costs!"

He strode out to the Hillman Minx, waiting at the kerb, and a minute later was humming down Main Street as fast as the traffic of that congested thoroughfare would allow.

In his urgent dash to the docks, Blake passed within fifty yards of the cafe in the casemates where A. J. Raffles awaited the coming of darkness.

CHAPTER 15

THEY HANG THEM IN GIBRALTAR

IT was long in coming, that darkness. Even when the sunlight began to fade from the square opening in the casemate wall, and the lights were switched on, there remained—for Raffles—hours to kill. About eight o'clock, the Cafe Obrero began to fill up with cocheros and taxi-drivers and guides. A big liner's arrival made a good day for these people, and the Italian *Rex*—which had come in a little before noon, and had left again at seven-thirty, for Genoa—is the biggest of the liners which call regularly at Gibraltar.

The Cafe Obrero's clientele had money to spend to-night. The tunnel in the casemates became crowded and noisy, the dice-boxes rattled, furious arguments broke out at this table and that, the air became thick with the fumes of aguardiente and Manzanilla, clouds of tobacco-smoke drifted up toward the electric bulbs pendant among the hams, the strings of onions, sausages and bleached garlic. You could have cut the atmosphere with a knife.

Three villainous-looking tourist-guides took the spare chairs at Raffles' table, ordered wine, produced a pack of greasy cards and their bankrolls—mostly in U.S. dollar bills—and began to play a game they called El Diablo. Through his tinted glasses, the "Hindu" watched a couple of hands played, saw that the game was merely vingt-et-un, and, producing a handful of notes, asked to join the game.

On the stroke of eleven, a policeman came in. Looking strangely incongruous in his London bobby's uniform and helmet, he accepted a glass of wine from the proprietor, drank it, and in a stentorian voice announced:

"Tiempo, tiempo! Anda, hombres—anda, todos!"

Closing time!

"Ram Dass" went out with the wrangling and noisy crowd. His parting from the three cut-throat tourist-guides lacked—on their side—cordiality. Their plunder from the *Rex's* passengers was down by approximately forty dollars. The "Hindu" with the studious-looking dark glasses knew his vingt-et-un!

Any idea, however, which the three baffled cut-throats may have entertained of waylaying "Ram Dass", and sticking him up for his winnings, was doomed to disappointment. The "Hindu" did not linger in the quarrelling group in the moonlight outside the casement cafe. Nobody saw him go. He just vanished.

He vanished, as a matter of fact, into the network of dark, narrow alleys behind Irish Town. When he came to a convenient doorway, he ducked into it, sat down on the step, lighted a cigarette.

The clock of the English cathedral chimed two short notes. Eleven-thirty. It was stiflingly hot in these alleys behind Irish Town; both air and moonlight were cut off by the high, narrow, shuttered warehouses. But after the atmosphere of the Cafe Obrero, the air here seemed positively limpid, the silence was a boon.

Raffles finished his cigarette without haste. After this, he took Bunny's automatic from his pocket, made sure that it was loaded.

Five minutes later, he was in the deserted cross-street called "Irish Town", standing in front of the shuttered shop marked Paneria, peering up the dark alley on one side of which was Chundra's backyard, on the other side of which was the Bar Monte Cristo. All quiet. Along Main Street, which cut across the top end of the alley, a horse-carriage went past, the clip-clop of the horse's hoofs ringing hollow.

When the sound of the carriage had faded into silence, Raffles moved quickly, silent as a shadow, up the alley, hugging the wall on Chundra's side. He saw nobody. He heard no suspicious sound. He reached that part of the whitewashed wall which, as described to him by Bunny, flanked the Hindu's backyard. He stood motionless for some seconds, listening. The sound of a small squad of men, marching in heavy boots, reached him from Main Street—naval pickets, he guessed, returning to their ship.

The pickets went by.

The moment they had passed, Raffles turned, reached up, caught the top of the wall. He scaled it easily, dropped lightly down on the inside.

Listening, holding his breath, he heard a faint whistle, somewhere close. He answered it. Bunny's voice came out of the darkness:

"Straight ahead!"

Raffles moved forward a few paces, very cautiously— and a hand caught his arm in the darkness, pulling him down. "All clear," Bunny whispered. "Dan and I've been here about five minutes. We slipped up through the alleys round Irish Town. No sign of cops on the watch anywhere, and all quiet in the store here."

"Then I'm going in," Raffles breathed. "You two stay here. You may be needed. You may not. If Drusilla's in the place, and she's alive, and I can get her out on my own, I shall—and turn her over to you here. After that, don't wonder what's happened to me. I shall vanish. If all goes well, you won't see me again for weeks, perhaps." He went on: "If I can't get her out on my own, if I'm hard-pressed, I shall whistle you from the nearest window. It's up to you boys, then, to get in somehow—but no shooting unless you're forced to it; a shot'd rouse the town. Use your butts."

Bunny nodded in the darkness. "Good luck!"

Raffles felt his way round the pile of old packing-cases behind which Bunny and the young American were crouched. He was going, he thought sardonically to need good luck—lots of it.

He made his way cautiously across the yard. Everything was pitch black. The back of the building showed no lights, but high up the moonlight silvered the roof and showed a shuttered dark window in the top storey.

Down here in the backyard, Raffles found the rear door of the building by the elementary process of bumping into it. He waited a moment, listening—then rapped quietly on the door with his knuckles. He rapped several times, listening between the raps. There was no sound within. He dared not rap louder. He left the door and, seeking a window, groped along the wall to his left. His fingers encountered the slats of shutters. He felt for the division between the shutters, took a penknife from his pocket, and went to work on the catch.

A few seconds, and with a snap the catch went back. He hooked his fingers through a slat, pulled on it gently. He expected to feel the resistance of an upper catch, but the shutters drew open. And as they opened, through the window behind them—which was also open—an arm snaked out, and the hard muzzle of an automatic jarred Raffles' chest.

A voice spoke in sibilant, spitting Hindustani.

Stockstill, with that gun against his chest, Raffles spoke in English. "It is I—Ram Dass!"

"Raffles!" came the sibilant exclamation. "Enter!"

The gun was withdrawn. Raffles put a leg over the

sill, ducked into the black room. He heard the shutters drawn to behind him, the creak of a sashcord as the window was closed, the rattle of brass rings as the curtains were pulled together.

Then a light snapped on. The dark glasses prevented his eyes from being dazzled. He saw that there were four Hindus in the room, none of whom was Lal Chundra.

One of the Hindus, thick-set, pock-marked, an automatic in his hand, smiled with a flash of white teeth.

"It iss well. Ever since dark we have been expecting you. We heard your rapping, but Chundra instructed us not to answer. If it were you, he said, you would force a window. Why did you not come earlier?"

"I couldn't," Raffles said briefly.

"Danger? Oah, assuredlee there is danger tonight—everywhere there iss danger! Come! Chundra awaits you."

The young-old, slender Hindu sat on a pouffe in that lofty, quiet Oriental room over the store. He did not move when Raffles was brought in through the door hung with a prayer-rug. The Hindu's slim hands, with the yellow half-moons in the nails, hung lax between his knees. His dark, brilliant eyes surveyed the cracksman.

"How iss this?" Lal Chundra said, without preamble. "How iss this that you have again assumed the 'Ram Dass' disguise?"

Raffles took off his dark glasses. His blue, keen eyes met the brilliant gaze of the Hindu.

"What do you mean—'again'? I've never abandoned it. You know what happened last night at the burning-ghats?"

"I know."

"I got away by the skin of my teeth. I've been in hiding ever since. I came here as soon as I dared. We made a bargain. You want the Weyman Manuscript. To get it you undertook to smuggle me out of Gibraltar——"

"Stop!" said Lal Chundra with a sudden, fierce gesture. His eyes held a dark glow. His voice had lost its silken suavity. "You say you have never abandoned your 'Ram Dass' disguise?"

"You can see for yourself——" Raffles began, but the Hindu stopped him.

"You were not thus disguised when you signalled me from the Bar Monte Cristo this afternoon, and I conveyed to you an order to stay away from the store here until after dark."

Raffles' own blank astonishment seemed to infect the Hindu. His voice rose.

"But it was you who signalled me from the Bar Monte Cristo, was it not? And yet——" He was on his feet suddenly. "Your expression betrays you! It was not you in the bar——"

"No!" Raffles said explosively. "It was not! I've been nowhere near the place till I came here a few minutes ago. I don't know what you're talking about. If somebody you thought was me signalled you from the Bar Monte Cristo this afternoon——"

He broke off. Like a thunderclap understanding came to him. Chundra had been tricked. He had been taken in by a ruse. This was Blake's work. Raffles recognised instantly the hand of the crafty, astute criminologist. Suspecting Chundra of being in with Raffles, Blake had tested his suspicions by posing as Raffles and signalling Chundra. By answering the signal, Chundra had betrayed himself!

But why hadn't Blake arrested him on the spot? There could be only one answer; Blake had judged that Raffles would return to the Hindu store for shelter. That meant, for certain, not merely that the store was watched, but that Blake had thrown a concealed cordon round it!

Raffles and the Hindu faced each other. Realisation had come simultaneously to them both. The significance of their position was glaring. They had been out-manoeuvred by a cleverer man. They were trapped!

In the light of the big Moorish chandelier over his head, the Hindu's dark face had a yellowish tinge. His eyes, with a dark glow in them, roved with a hunted look over the walls of the room. His red tongue flickered along his dry, dark lips.

"You realise what this means?"

"It's plain enough, isn't it?" Raffles said. "You killed Marius to put me in a murder jam, and now you're caught in it yourself! The police—Blake—Blake of Baker Street, Chundra—will be here at any minute. He'll find the American girl. You've got her here, Chundra, and I know it. You kidnapped her because she witnessed the killing of Marius. When Blake finds her, her testimony'll clear me of that crime, at any rate—but, by heaven, it'll hang you and your stiletto expert!"

The pock-marked Hindu who stood behind Raffles moved forward suddenly, but Lal Chundra checked him with a gesture.

"Wait, Mukerji! Raffles, you are right. If I am taken I have no chance. Was it not I myself who said to you: 'They hang in Gibraltar!' " Suavity had come back into the Hindu's voice. "But, if you are taken, you will not get off lightly yourself, Raffles. In my safe is your 'Bell-Evart' passport, which you left with me. For that forgery, if on no other charge, Blake—oh, yes, I knew who had succeeded Sacarello—Blake can incarcerate you for seven years. You cannot afford to be taken any more than I can. But do you think that I, who have a hand in very many dangerous games, am without loopholes of escape? There is a way out for us both—and for Mukerji here, who threw the stiletto. You will see. Wait, both of you! See that he does not move, Mukerji!"

Chundra crossed quickly to the prayer-rug which concealed the door. Watching closely, Raffles saw this time how that door was operated from within. To the left of it was a niche in the wall; in the niche stood a small vase with an ebony base. Chundra's slender fingers lightly brushed the base of the vase, giving it a slight turn to the right, and behind the prayer-rug the door swung open unseen.

Chundra vanished, the prayer-rug swinging back into place behind him.

Raffles looked at Mukerji. The pock-marked Hindu was watching him narrowly, his small automatic pointed steadily at Raffles' chest.

"You will not move, Raffles. You heard Lal Chundra's order."

"I heard it," Raffles said, "and I'll tell you something, Mukerji. You're going to hang, and I'm going to prison! And shall I tell you why, Mukerji? Because he'll double-cross us! He's got a loophole all right, and he's headed for it now. But d'you think he'll come back for us? Not a cat's chance!"

He saw the Hindu's eyes flicker with a sudden, sharp suspicion towards the door, and he went on smoothly:

"That's what's going to happen to you and me, Mukerji! We're going to be left holding the bag!"

With the word "bag" Raffles' right arm shot forward like a piston, his fist took the Hindu on the point of the jaw, and Mukerji went down like a man poleaxed.

Raffles rushed the door. He ripped down the prayer-rug with his right hand, with his left gave a quick turn to the ebony base of the vase in the niche. There was a faint whir, a click, and the door swung open.

Raffles stepped out into the dark passage, stood listening. For a second this dark, faintly musk-smelling house was utterly silent—then from above, from some upper storey, there came the sound of a door slamming. So slight was the sound, though unmistakable in its origin, that Raffles judged it to have come from the top floor.

He moved a few paces into the darkness to his left, paused, struck a match. The light shone on his lean, dark-stained face, showed his eyes—he had dropped the tinted glasses—blue and glittering.

Before him was a narrow staircase, matting-covered, curving upward. The match burned his fingers, and, as he dropped it, through the silent house rang a peremptory hammering, as of a pistol-butt or a truncheon on a closed door.

Blake! The cordon had closed in!

There was no need now to worry about Drusilla. Blake

would find her if she were here. For Raffles there was just one ghost of a chance of getting out of the trap into which he had walked. He must catch up with Chundra before the Hindu closed his loophole behind him.

Raffles groped his way forward up the dark, narrow, musty-smelling staircase. He moved swiftly. The darkness was impenetrable. He had no torch. But his expert cracksman's instinct seemed to sketch out in his mind the probable geography of this tall, narrow house.

Here he was on a landing. Along there to the right, he judged, there should be another staircase, going up. He moved along the landing, running a hand flat along the wall. His hand found a gap. Yes, here was the staircase!

As he mounted it, groping his way the rapping far below ceased abruptly; a second later there echoed through the silent house a shattering crash. A confusion of shouting voices came up to him, a scream, the detonation of a pistol.

He did not stop. He was in a closer corner than any into which Blake had forced him before. But he wasn't caught yet!

Another landing. Another staircase. He mounted swiftly. No, he was on yet another landing—much narrower, as his groping hands told him, than those below. This must be the top floor, from which had come that far-off door-slam.

He checked, breathing quickly, his heart hammering. Along the landing on his left he saw a thin line of light under a door. Quickly, silently, he moved towards it—heard a voice speak within:

"——so confident, my dear Miss Brook, that you will be able to clear him of the murder in the Monte Cristo!" The voice was Chundra's. "But he is mistaken there. For, if you are found dead, you can neither clear anybody nor accuse anybody. The dead cannot testify. Therefore my dear Miss Brook, before I leave——"

Raffles' groping fingers found the handle of the door. He turned the handle and threw his weight against the panels in one simultaneous movement.

The door flew open, precipitating him, off balance, into the room. Drusilla stood, slender, lovely, defiant, against the opposite wall. Chundra faced her, a little crouched, a naked stiletto gleaming in his hand.

He turned, quick as a panther, as the door flew open. The stiletto flashed up, an arc of silver fire—and Raffles' hand caught the Hindu's slender wrist in midair, twisted it savagely back. Chundra screamed in pain, bowing to his knees in the agony of that grip which threatened to break his arm. Raffles chopped down his right fist on the base of the Hindu's skull—a paralysing, numbing blow that dropped Chundra limp and unconscious at the cracksman's feet.

Raffles stepped across the Hindu towards the girl. She shrank from him, her grey eyes wide. He said urgently:

"It's all right—it's all right, Drusilla!"

"Major Bell-Evart!"

"Yes. Don't worry. You're out of the wood. They've come for you. Dan Westray's downstairs."

Her eyes searched his face. She said breathlessly:

"But you?"

Raffles smiled wryly. "They've come for me, too—the police! But they aren't going to get me!"

His eyes roved swiftly round the room. It was sparsely furnished with a camp-bed, a washstand, a couple of chairs, a desk, a small modern safe. There was no window, but in one wall of the room was a low, arched recess, like a fireplace that lacked both chimney and grate. But the recess had no back to it. Stooping, he saw through it the dull gleam of moonlight on the leads of a flat roof. He straightened, looking at the girl with a gleam of triumph in his eyes.

Drusilla Brook nodded.

"That's the way he was going! He moved a loose brick in the wall, just over there, and a sort of door opened in the back of the recess. This is the room I've been a prisoner in. I had no idea the door was there till a minute ago, when he worked it." She caught her breath.

"I can hear people downstairs. Go—quickly, major! Oh, quickly—quickly!"

He looked at her. "You want me to escape?"

"You've just saved my life," she said simply.

Raffles glanced at the safe. He stooped suddenly, with expert hand frisked the pockets of Lal Chundra's white duck coat, removed a bunch of keys and an automatic.

"In that safe," he said, "there's something I must have. It's a passport. It could get me seven years if I'm caught. Do you think that, with the aid of this toy"—he handed her the automatic—"you could prevent anybody from coming up here for, say, three to four minutes? Hold them up—pretend not to believe their bona fides—be difficult to convince? Could you do that?"

She drew a long breath, looking at him, her eyes sparkling. "Trust me, major, and—good luck!"

She held out her hand. Raffles took it, raised it to his lips.

"Good luck, Drusilla Brook!"

Then she was gone. The door closed behind her.

Raffles stepped quickly to the safe, went down on one knee before it. His lean, strong, sensitive fingers turned the dial of the combination with the touch of a master.

CHAPTER 16

EXHIBITS A TO Z

What happened to Raffles after he left them behind that pile of packing-cases in the darkness of Chundra's backyard, Messrs. Bunny Manders and Dan Westray had no means of knowing.

What happened to themselves, after some tense minutes of waiting, was disaster.

It came without warning. No sound heralded it. At one moment they were crouching in pitch blackness behind that pile of packing-cases. At the next, four powerful electric torches were blazing into their eyes from the top of the wall which divided the backyard from the alley.

A voice—Blake's voice—rasped:

"Stand up! Raise your hands, and keep them raised!"

They were helpless. There was no choice but to obey. Blinded by the concentrated glare of those four torches, the two men rose, their hands above their heads.

Dazzled, Bunny could not see Blake's face, but he heard the detective's voice:

"Put the bracelets on them, inspector. Send them back to headquarters. Manders, this is quite a satisfaction to me. I suppose you'll deny that Raffles is in this house here?"

Bunny moistened his lips. His voice was cool, almost insolent:

"I don't know what you're talking about! Raffles? The last I heard of Raffles, he was in Honolulu!"

Blake chuckled, in the darkness behind his torch.

"Then it's going to be a pleasant surprise for you when I bring A. J. along presently to share your cell! Take 'em away, inspector!"

Blake turned his attention to the back door of the building. Running the blazing circle of his flash-lamp over the door, he moved forward to it.

"Give them a knock, sergeant!"

The mountainous Sergeant Mifsud, in white ducks instead of his more usual uniform, drew a squat truncheon from his pocket, hammered on the door with it, paused to listen. There was no sound within the building.

"Again!" Blake said.

Mifsud hammered again on the door. Still there was no answer.

"All right," Blake said. "Sergeant, you're developed in build. Let's see what you can do with your shoulder!"

The dusky sergeant drew back, grinning, and catapulted himself at the door like a human battering-ram. Few doors could have withstood the shock of that nineteen-stone assault. This one gave at the hinges. It crashed inward, with the huge bulk of Sergeant Mifsud sprawling on top of it; and Blake's torch, blazing along a narrow passage, arrested three white-clad Hindus in the act of mounting a flight of stairs. One of the Hindus wheeled round, shouting, his hand whipping up with the flash of a knife in it.

Blake's automatic spoke crisply. The Hindu pitched forward down the stairs. The other two, grey-faced in the white blaze of the flash-lamp, crouched on the stairs with raised hands.

"That's better," Blake said. "Hoik 'em out of that, sergeant!"

The enormous policeman "hoiked" them out, as requested, with a hand on the collar of each.

Blake, Tinker at his heels, stepped over the shot man, and, throwing the light of his torch ahead of him, went on up the stairs.

So he came to the room over the store. The door of this room stood open, hitching back the prayer-rug. On the floor lay a man, in the inevitable white ducks of the Hindu, face down.

This room was lighted by a huge, Moorish chandelier. Blake snapped out his torch, dropped it into a pocket of his blue, double-breasted coat, went down on one knee beside the Hindu. He turned him over, sliding a hand inside his shirt. Then he smiled, glancing up at Tinker, pointed to a purpling bruise under the dusky skin of the man's pockmarked jaw.

"Our left-hook expert again," Blake said. "The Raffles touch! I think we have Raffles cold this time, Tinker! The cordon's tight round the place. He can't get out. Let's try the next floor."

Stepping out again into the dark passage, he flashed his torch up a narrow, curving staircase. He started up the stairs, Tinker, Captain Adam, and Sergeant Mifsud following.

Blake was halfway up the stairs when a slender figure in white appeared suddenly at the head of the staircase.

Simultaneously, a light was snapped on, up there on the landing, and a quiet voice said:

"I shouldn't come any farther, if I were you!"

Blake said pleasantly: "Miss Drusilla Brook, I believe?"

"That's my name."

"We are the police!"

She faced them coolly, her weapon in her small, brown hand. "How am I to know that? You are not uniformed. How am I to know that you are not more of Chundra's creatures?"

Blake took a step forward up the stairs. Drusilla's voice, crisp, decisive, checked him instantly:

"I shan't warn you again! One more step, and it'll be your last! I mean that!"

With his bandaged hand, Blake twitched back the lapel of his coat, showing a Gibraltar Police badge. He spoke with a sudden icy harshness:

"I'm arresting you, Drusilla Brook, for the theft of the Weyman Manuscript from Forge Park, Westchester County, on the night of January the fifteenth! Here"— from his breast-pocket he whipped a small, thick, black-covered exercise-book secured by a leather strap—"here is the Weyman Manuscript, which I found tonight in a locked attache-case in your cabin on the *Llandnno Ch*——"

He broke off, springing forward up the stairs as the girl, deathly white, closed her eyes, swayed, fell.

"Take her, captain! Careful—careful——"

"I've got her," said the Army sleuth.

"Come on you others!" Blake rapped.

A big, flat, blue-steel automatic gleamed dully in his hand as he raced forward along the landing. He threw open door after door.

"Nothing doing! Next floor! They're here somewhere —Raffles and Chundra!"

He mounted the stairs with long strides, Tinker at his heels, the mountainous Mifsud lumbering in the rear.

On the top floor, he saw instantly the line of light under the door at the end of the landing. He raced along to the door, hurled it open—stopped dead.

Lal Chundra lay sprawled on his back on the floor, unconscious. On the upturned palm of his limp right hand lay a slender, vicious-looking stiletto, its ivory hilt carved into the likeness of an elephant's head and trunk. Scattered all about him were papers, letters, documents. Against one wall stood a small safe with its door yawning open. Directly opposite Blake was a small washstand with a wall-mirror over it. The mirror reflected him, there in the doorway, with Tinker and Mifsud behind him. Scrawled across the mirror, in huge, white capitals, written in soap, was a message:

BLAKE, WITH COMPLIMENTS!
EXHIBITS A TO Z.
ADIOS!

A. J. Raffles, alias Major Alan Bell-Evart, had vanished!

. . . . .

Some twenty-five minutes later, right over on the other side of the Rock, a figure ducked through the rails of the racecourse, on the Mediterranean side, where the belt of eucalyptus trees grew.

All quiet in the refugee encampment. Here and there, in the pitch darkness under the shadow of the mighty precipice which faces Spain, glowed the red sparks of dying camp-fires, the fading gleam of exhausted naphtha flares.

The prowling figure of the amateur cracksman gave these a wide berth; and of all the three thousand pairs of eyes in that camp of war waifs, one pair only spotted that swift, stealthy figure flitting through the camp.

These were the eyes of Emilio Roca, sitting cross-legged on his blankets, the red spark of a cigarette occasionally glowing up to show shadowily his lean, lined face and dark, hot eyes.

He saw the figure approaching. As it came close, he whispered sibilantly:

"Ram Dass?"

"Si, si!"

Next second, Raffles ducked into the tent. He sat down. For some seconds, breathing hard, he did not speak. Roca rolled a cigarette, handed it to the "Hindu", thrust against it the spark of his own cigarette, for Raffles to light up from.

The cracksman inhaled deeply, filling his lungs with smoke. He gestured toward the prone forms of the other men in the tent. "They sleep?"

Roca nodded.

"I waited for you. I have had news. Papers have been issued to those who are to leave in the *Wild Swan*—also, these tabs, see, which we tie to our buttonholes. The destroyer is to sail at dawn. We who leave are to gather at the racecourse buildings at four a.m. Lo siento, Ram Dass, none of the Hindus in the camp are of the number!"

"I see," Raffles said softly. "Who else in this tent goes, beside you?"

"Miguel Gamboa."

Raffles took from his pocket a thick wad of Gibraltar one-pound notes. He struck a match, so that the small, fierce Spaniard could see them.

"There is here one hundred and fifty pounds sterling," Raffles said softly. "I will give this to the man who will let me use his papers, clothes, and buttonhole tag and go aboard the *Wild Swan* in his place. It will take the destroyer at most thirty hours to reach Valencia. The man who sells me his things can slip out from the racecourse before four a.m., lie under cover in the town for thirty hours, then go to the police, say that he was kidnapped, smuggled out of the camp, his papers, clothes, and tag taken from him. He can say that he was taken blindfold to some house, in which he was held prisoner for thirty hours; that at the end of that time he was led, blindfold, away from the house by a roundabout route, and released in the town. He can say that he came straight to the police—that he cannot hope to find the house where he was held. You follow me? The police could prove nothing!

No harm could come to the man, and—I will pay one hundred and fifty pounds!"

. . . . .

Just over half a mile away, in police headquarters, Blake sat at the desk of the late Inspector Sacarello. Present were Drusilla Brook, Bunny Manders, and Dan Westray, Andrew Payne Hulburd—whom Blake had summoned by telephone—Captain Adam, and Inspector Parodi.

Chundra was still unconscious, in a prison cell. Mukerji had confessed to throwing, under Chundra's orders, the stiletto which had killed Marius; he had further confessed that the murder of Sacarello had been committed at Chundra's order.

On the blotting-pad in front of Blake lay the thick, black, strapped-up exercise-book which was the manuscript of John Drake Weyman.

Blake said briefly.

"The conversation between yourself and your stepson, Mr. Hulburd, was overheard by my assistant. That conversation completed my solution. I was already certain that a robbery had occurred at Forge Park on January 15th which you had chosen to hush up. I thought 'Bell-Evart' was the thief, and that Marius was a man employed by you to recover what 'Bell-Evart' had stolen.

"The conversation thus overheard changed my views. It revealed that Westray here was your stepson, that at your instigation he was following and trying to 'contact' Miss Brook. For what purpose? I could think only of one —namely, that he was trying to recover that which had been stolen from Forge Park. If this were so, then Miss Brook was the thief, and not Bell-Evart. I therefore stopped the *Llandnno Chief*'s sailing, and searched Miss Brook's cabin. I found—this!"

He touched the manuscript.

"The complete formula, devised by one John Drake Weyman, for the manufacture of an astonishingly cheap and effective synthetic fuel for internal combustion engines—together with his complete and exhaustive notes upon the process. It was plain to me, at once, that this was what had been stolen from Forge Park. It was equally plain that Miss Brook was the thief!

"Now, Chundra held Miss Brook a prisoner because she witnessed the murder of Marius. (Marius, we now know, was Chundra's own man.) But Chundra believed Bell-Evart to be the thief who had stolen the Weyman Manuscript. Although Chundra held Miss Brook, he had no idea that she, and not Bell-Evart, was in possession of the Weyman Manuscript. In short, the whole time he held Miss Brook, Chundra as good as had the Weyman Manuscript in his hands—and he didn't know it. He was contriving elaborate devices to try to get it from Bell-Evart."

The tall, white-haired old American said quietly:

"Mr. Blake, I tried to hush the Forge Park theft up. You see, I was pretty certain who had stolen the manuscript. Miss Brook is John Drake Weyman's niece. Weyman came to me with the request that I finance his experiments. I did so gladly. I allotted him a laboratory on my Forge Park estate. I took an interest in his progress. But Weyman suffered from a persecution complex. He misconstrued my interest. He thought I designed to steal his formula. He wrote his niece of his suspicions; he warned her that if anything happened to him, I should be responsible for it. She loved her uncle; she believed what he said. Unfortunately, he died—suddenly. Miss Brook, not unnaturally, believed the worst. I tried to get in touch with her, but she had vanished from her home in San Francisco.

"Shortly afterwards, on the night of January 15th, Weyman's manuscript was stolen from my safe. Do you wonder that I suspected her, but that I hushed the robbery up? Do you wonder—knowing that there were people in the world who had heard of Weyman's experiments, and would not stop at murder to obtain his formula —that I set my stepson to trace her, to protect her, to try to get her confidence, make her understand that I was her friend, not her enemy?"

183

Blake leaned back in his desk chair, his brown, long fingers loading his pipe.

"Yes, Mr. Hulburd!" the criminologist said quietly, "I well understand why you hushed up the robbery; I well understand why you were anxious for Miss Brook's safety, with such a document in her possession. This other document here"—he touched a paper on his desk—"obligingly taken from Chundra's safe by Bell-Evart, and left by him for me to find, alone shows you had good reason for anxiety. It shows that one of the totalitarian states—never mind which—commissioned Chundra to get the Weyman Manuscript by any means whatever. If he got it, he was to receive for it the sum of one million pounds!"

He lighted his pipe.

"It's plain that this world-wide chain of tourist-traps that calls itself Chundra, Khitagara and Co. is mixed up in espionage and international politics of all kinds. Getting Lal Chundra—he'll hang, of course—doesn't mean that we can close these stores; but it means the company will be frightened into dropping its illicit business for quite a long time to come!"

Drusilla Brook said quietly:

"I've been a fool. What Mr. Hulburd calls my uncle's 'persecution complex' led me into this. I did not actually steal the manuscript myself. I employed a certain Chicago safebreaker to do it for me. Major Bell-Evart was certainly at Forge Park that night. The crook I employed saw him and recognised him as an Englishman who was staying in the neighbourhood. Then I heard, from an officer of the *Llandnno Chief*, at Aden—I had gone to Aden to see a certain man whom my uncle had told me was a likely buyer of the manuscript—that they had a Major Alan Bell-Evart on board, under arrest for a robbery at Forge Park. I got this bit of news quite by chance. I felt a sense of guilt; I felt that Major Bell-Evart had been arrested for a crime I was responsible for. I hurried to Port Said and joined the ship there. I didn't quite know what I hoped to do, but——"

She drew a long breath and looked at Dan Westray—and the lean, brown, blond-haired young American smiled. Blake, watching, read the look in Dan's eyes—and the answering look in Drusilla's. The criminologist glanced at Andrew Payne Hulburd.

"I take it," Blake said, "that you don't charge Miss Brook with the Forge Park theft, Mr. Hulburd?"

"Of course not! Her uncle's formula is her own property."

"Then," Blake said, "I have no charge against her. She's free. Incidentally, when she sells the formula, she'll be worth something in the neighbourhood of a million pounds! Congratulations, Miss Brook!" He looked at Dan Westray. "I have no charge against you, Westray. You merely tried, in a rather ill-advised way, to rescue Miss Brook from kidnappers without the aid of the police."

Bunny Manders adjusted his eyeglass carefully. He beamed. "That goes for me, too, I think, Mr. Blake? I'm guilty only of assisting Westray."

Blake looked at him enigmatically.

"I have no charge to bring against you, Manders—unfortunately! You are free. But if I chance to meet Mr. Bell-Evart—well, it will probably be exceedingly awkward for you both!"

Seated on a coil of rope aboard a British destroyer sat A. J. Raffles. He fingered a wad of banknotes, and then a small washleather bag containing diamonds. The notes and the diamonds were from the safe of Lal Chundra!

A. J. Raffles—a judge of such things—estimated the value of the diamonds at not less than ten thousand pounds. With that, and the sure knowledge that there was no possible charge Blake could make against Bunny Manders, Raffles felt that he had some excuse to chuckle.

Blake might have solved the mystery and trapped Lal Chundra. Good for Blake! But he, Raffles, had got away with the doings. Good for Raffles!